Stellar's Fate

Part 1: The Genesis

Chirag Makwana

&

Yash Siddhpura

Introduction

Chirag Makwana

From the bustling streets of Mumbai, where the rhythm of life echoes in every corner, I present my debut novel. A culmination of my multifaceted journey, this book reflects my passions, my ambitions, and my unwavering belief in the power of storytelling. As a BCom graduate, a final year ACCA student, and a musician and filmmaker, my life has always been a vibrant tapestry woven with creativity and ambition. My father, a musician himself, instilled in me a deep love for music, which I later channeled into film composition for the short film "Kaali Panni." But it's my overthinking mind, my constant stream of ideas, that led me to storytelling. This book is a reflection of my journey, a peek into my world, and a testament to the transformative power of words. I hope it resonates with you, ignites your imagination, and leaves you wanting more.

Instagram: @chiragmakwanaaaa

Yash Siddhpura

I am a TE Computer Engineer pursuing web development and AI/ML. I aim to master computer languages through conceptual understanding and by creating practical projects. I am also a UPSC aspirant, an eloquent orator, a writer, and a motivational speaker sharing insights on YouTube. With discipline and values as my compass, I navigate through challenges with the spirit of a soldier and the brilliance of a genius. Passion fuels my ambitions, while dedication shapes my path. I am a gentleman by nature, inspiring others through my words and actions, embodying the essence of a true leader. Amidst it all, I also prioritize fitness, sculpting both my body and mind to achieve greatness. Additionally, I love to travel and explore new places, have new experiences, meet new people, and am always curious to learn. I enjoy building valuable bonds, friendships, and memories. With a positive mindset, I take charge of difficult situations and strive to find solutions. I do everything I can to help those who approach me when they are facing problems and guide them in their lives by showing them the right path.

Instagram: @yashsiddhpura_

Lavanya Vishwakarma

By profession I'm an IT engineer, but my heart belongs to the worlds I create with my drawings and lines of code. Inside these pages, you'll find a blend of my passions. These drawings are a special tribute to my mother, who always encouraged my creative spirit. I hope you enjoy the journey.

Instagram: @lavanya.vishu13_

Disclaimer

This novel is a work of fiction, and any resemblance to actual persons, living or dead, or actual events is purely coincidental. The author has taken creative liberties in crafting this story, drawing inspiration from the boundless possibilities of space exploration and the human imagination. While the novel delves into themes of space travel and interstellar encounters, it is important to emphasize that the scientific concepts presented are purely fictional and do not reflect established scientific theories or factual data. The author's intention is not to present a scientifically accurate depiction of space exploration but rather to create a compelling narrative that transports readers to a realm of wonder and possibility.

The characters, their relationships, and the events they encounter are all products of the author's imagination. No real-world individuals or organizations are intended to be represented by these fictional entities. Furthermore, the author holds no intention to offend or disparage any individual, group, religion, race, caste, organization, gender, or cultural belief. This novel is a celebration of creativity and imagination, aiming to provide readers with an immersive and engaging experience. It is meant to be enjoyed as a work of fiction, free from any claims of factual accuracy or real-world implications.

Motivation

Chirag's journey to writing this novel began with a spark of inspiration for a short film. He envisioned a captivating story set against the backdrop of space, a world of wonder and adventure that he yearned to bring to life. He even enlisted the help of a friend, eager to collaborate on this creative endeavor. However, fate had other plans, and the short film never materialized. Undeterred, Chirag realized that the story he had conceived deserved a wider canvas, a platform that could fully embrace its grandeur. He began to expand upon the initial concept, letting the story unfold in his mind, taking shape and evolving over months of meticulous contemplation. The story grew, becoming more intricate and complex, ultimately demanding a larger scope than a short film could accommodate. Chirag recognized that the narrative he was crafting was destined to be a trilogy, a sprawling saga that would immerse readers in a captivating universe of his own creation. With this realization, he knew he needed a trusted collaborator, someone who shared his vision and passion for storytelling. He turned to Yash, his closest friend, a kindred spirit who understood his creative process and possessed a similar mindset when it came to crafting captivating narratives. Chirag poured his heart and soul into narrating the story to Yash, sharing every detail, every twist, every emotional nuance. Yash was captivated, recognizing the brilliance and potential of Chirag's creation. He readily agreed to join forces, and together they embarked on a ten-month odyssey of collaborative writing.

Through countless hours of dedicated work, fueled by shared passion and unwavering determination, Chirag and Yash brought their extraordinary vision to life. The result is a space adventure unlike any other, a captivating exploration of a universe teeming with wonder and possibility. This novel is a testament to their shared dedication, a culmination of their creative synergy, and a gift to readers who seek immersive experiences that ignite the imagination.

Table of Contents

<u>CHAPTERS</u>

1.

A Whisper

In

The Dark

In Norway, among a group of students, there is a boy named Rachit who is 23 years old. He has come to Norway to pursue further studies and has settled here. Rachit originally hails from Mumbai, India, where he lives with his mother, Tara. Since Rachit's birth, Tara has been a single mother, and Rachit has never known the identity of his father, as his mother has never disclosed this information to him. Despite this, Tara has raised Rachit as a hardworking individual.

Rachit has been in Norway for about six months now. Rachit has never been very social since childhood, which is why he spent most of his time with his mother. As a result, he is feeling quite lonely in Norway. His mother was aware of Rachit's social tendencies, and that's why she intentionally encouraged him to befriend someone named Yash. After his mother, Rachit shares the strongest bond with his friend Yash, whom he met for the first time in school. They have remained close friends ever since, but lately, due to their focus on careers and the challenges of living in a different country, their conversations have become less frequent. Otherwise, they used to share everything and couldn't go a day without talking to each other.

Rachit has always been a bright student, and because of this, his mother dreamed of him attending a prestigious university and becoming a successful individual. To ensure that his talent would not go to waste, she sent him to Norway for his studies. Currently, Rachit hasn't made any close friends; his interactions are mostly limited to college projects or with his roommate, Ryan. During the rest of his time, he prefers to be alone. His studies and household chores consume so much of his time that, despite wanting to, he hasn't been able to form friendships with anyone.

And so, the story begins…

Rachit is sitting in a large lecture hall at his university, fully focused on his studies. He is taking notes and understanding the methods being explained by the professor. Suddenly, the bell rings, signalling the end of the day and the last lecture. Rachit and the other students start packing their bags and leaving the classroom one by one. Rachit is the last to leave, and as he passes by the professor, the professor calls out to him, "Rachit, come here."

Rachit approaches him and asks, "What, sir?"

The professor then says, "Happy Birthday, Rachit!"

Rachit is a bit surprised to hear this and asks, "How did you know, sir?"

The professor replies, "I received notifications of everyone's birthdays in my data. You work hard and don't waste time, so I wanted to wish you privately; otherwise, I would have announced it in front of the whole class. Did I make any mistake?"

Rachit responds, "No, no, not at all, sir. You did the right thing, and thank you so much!" Being Indian, he then touches his professor's feet as a sign of respect before leaving the college, heading to the apartment where he lives with Ryan, who was also accommodated through the college.

Rachit steps outside his college and stops at the bus stop. He starts to take out his earphones to listen to music. At that moment, a car comes to a halt in front of him due to traffic. Rachit notices that a boy in the car is heading out to celebrate a birthday with his family. Seeing this makes Rachit feel quite sad because today is his birthday, and he has no one with him. So far, his mother hasn't even tried to contact him, and Rachit doesn't want to remind her that it's his birthday. At the same time, he hasn't received any messages from Yash wishing him a happy birthday either. As the traffic clears, the car moves past Rachit, and he tries to forget all of this. He puts his earphones back in and starts listening to music while waiting for the bus.

Suddenly, he notices a light shining somewhere, which catches his attention. A little further away, he sees a shadowy figure that looks like a completely black male figure peeking from behind a wall. Rachit finds this figure a bit strange because it looks like a full shadow. He feels a bit confused and wonders what this figure is, but he doesn't dwell on it for long and gets busy listening to his music.

Rachit boards the bus and settles into his favourite left window seat at the back, just like always. He leans over to look out the window, trying to catch a glimpse of that strange shadow he saw earlier, but it's gone now. Understanding that it was just a trick of his mind, he pushes the thought aside as the bus begins to move. As the bus glides through the beautiful city, Rachit is mesmerized by the stunning views that remind him of Norway. The scenery is so captivating that he feels as if the bus could wander through these picturesque streets for a lifetime.

After a few stops, the bus passes by a supermarket, and suddenly, Rachit remembers that his flat is running low on groceries. Realizing he needs to pick up some essentials, he quickly gets up from his seat and approaches the bus driver, asking if he could be dropped off there. The driver agrees, and Rachit is grateful as he steps off the bus, ready to grab what he needs before heading back home.

The atmosphere in the supermarket is quite subdued, with only a few shoppers around due to it being a weekday, accompanied by the staff who are busy attending to their tasks. Rachit begins to gather his essentials, pushing a basket along as he moves through the aisles. After about 15 minutes of browsing and selecting items, he finds himself at the very last row of the supermarket, where there's hardly anyone around. As he stands there, lost in thought, the lights in the supermarket flicker on and off, which strikes Rachit as odd. He starts to glance around, trying to figure out what's happening.

Suddenly, at a distance, he spots a figure that resembles the strange shadow he had seen before. This time, however, he is able to see it more clearly. The figure appears shadowy, but upon closer inspection, Rachit notices small, shimmering white dots scattered across its form. Intrigued and slightly unnerved, he continues to observe, wondering what this mysterious presence could be.

Rachit, in a panic, starts to step back, his voice trembling as he pleads, "Don't come near me!" The shadowy figure begins to move slowly towards him, and fear grips Rachit as he shouts for help, "Help! Help!" He turns and starts to run in the opposite direction, trying to escape the advancing presence. The shadowy figure quickens its pace, closing the distance between them. In his haste, Rachit trips over his basket, falling to the ground and screaming loudly. As he looks up, the shadow leaps directly towards him.

Suddenly, everything around him turns dark, and he sees only the faint glimmer of small, white dots. Just then, he feels a firm hand on his shoulder, and he realizes he is back in the supermarket, lying on the floor. A staff member stands over him, concern etched on his face. "Sir, are you okay? I heard your screams and rushed over. Did something happen to you?"

Taking a moment to calm himself, Rachit gathers the items he managed to collect and heads to the checkout. After paying, he quickly steps outside, hailing a taxi to head back to his flat, still shaken by the experience.

The taxi driver notices Rachit's troubled expression and asks, "What's wrong, sir? You look really worried. Is there a problem?"

Rachit replies, "I don't know, but since this morning, I've been seeing some strange visuals. There's been this shadowy figure that keeps appearing, and it all escalated when it jumped right over me, plunging me into darkness for a moment.

Then a staff member at the supermarket brought me back to my senses, and I just panicked and ran out."

Listening intently, the taxi driver responds, "Sir, do you live here alone? You don't seem like you're from around here."

Rachit answers, "Yes, I'm here for my further studies. I came from India."

The driver then suggests, "Maybe you're experiencing some mental strain. If you're feeling homesick and you're alone here, it's possible that you're just a bit overwhelmed, which could be causing these hallucinations."

Rachit considers this perspective and feels a sense of relief wash over him, realizing that perhaps the driver's insight might hold some truth. The taxi comes to a stop in front of Rachit's apartment. He pays the driver and expresses his gratitude for the conversation they had.

As Rachit starts to walk towards the entrance of his building, the taxi driver calls out, "Sir, come here!"

Curious, Rachit approaches the taxi and asks, "What happened?"

The driver rummages through the rear shelf of his car and, after a moment, pulls out a card. He hands it to Rachit and explains, "A psychologist once sat in my car and gave me this card. I thought it might be helpful for you."

Rachit takes the card, thanking the driver sincerely for his thoughtfulness before heading into his apartment, feeling a little more hopeful.

Rachit lives in a five-story apartment building that is secured with a lock at the entrance, accessible only to the residents who have the key. Generally, not many people come and go from this apartment, which adds to the sense of isolation. Rachit's flat is on the fourth floor, and he doesn't enjoy the solitude of the place at all. The daily climb of four flights of stairs is something he truly dislikes. Feeling exhausted and overwhelmed, Rachit finally enters his room. He switches on the lights, illuminating the space that feels painfully empty, echoing his own sense of loneliness.

As he sits there, a wave of disappointment washes over him. It's his birthday, yet he hasn't received any wishes from his friends, especially Yash, or even from his mother. The silence in the apartment amplifies his feelings of neglect, deepening his sense of despair.

Despite the disappointment, he proceeded to prepare his meal while also organizing his bag for the next day's classes and setting aside clothes for laundry. As the clock neared nine in the evening, his hopes of receiving a birthday call began to fade. Seated at the table, taking a solitary meal, Rachit's gaze wandered out of the window, and to his surprise, he was greeted by the mesmerizing sight of the aurora dancing in the night sky. The ethereal display of colours painted across the darkness brought a moment of awe and wonder, offering a glimmer of beauty and solace in the midst of his subdued birthday evening.

As the chilly December night enveloped Rachit, the familiar dance of the aurora borealis painted the sky in hues of green, purple, and pink. Despite the bittersweet feeling of his mom forgetting his birthday, the cosmic display above offered a sense of belonging to something greater. The tranquil beauty of the lights cast a spell of peace and wonder, momentarily lifting his spirits and filling his heart with joy. Lost in the enchanting spectacle, Rachit spent nearly an hour captivated by the celestial show. When the lights eventually faded into the night, he rose from the table and checked his phone once more, hoping for a missed call or a message that never came, leaving a tinge of sadness in its wake. With a heavy heart, he proceeded to prepare for bed. After a soothing shower, Rachit settled onto his bed, the melody of a song his mother used to sing to him lingering in his mind. As he softly hummed the familiar tune, memories of warmth and comfort wrapped around him, offering solace in the quiet of the night.

The sudden ringing of his phone in the quiet of the night startled Rachit as he was on the brink of sleep. The unexpected sound broke the serene stillness, sending a shiver down his spine as he cautiously reached for his phone, unsure of what awaited on the other end. The dim glow of the screen illuminated the room, casting shadows that seemed to dance in the darkness, adding to the sense of apprehension that enveloped him.

Fig 1. Rachit gazed out his window, mesmerized by the aurora lights dancing across the sky.

2.

A Birthday Surprise Or A Nightmare?

On a calm and chilly night, Rachit was slowly drifting into a deep sleep when suddenly, breaking the serene atmosphere, his phone rang. He jolted awake as if he had just experienced a terrible nightmare. For a moment, his heart raced, pounding in his chest. He picked up his phone and saw that the call was from an unknown number. Given the strange occurrences that had happened to him earlier that day, he felt an unsettling fear creeping in, forcing his mind to wrestle with the decision of whether to answer the call or not.

Just as Rachit was about to make a choice, the ringtone stopped. He let out a sigh of relief, feeling as if a looming threat had passed him by. However, this moment of peace was fleeting, as his phone began to ring again from the same number that had called before. Gathering his courage, Rachit decided to answer the call this time.

Rachit spoke into the phone, "Hello? Who is this?"

For a moment, there was silence on the other end. He repeated, "Hello?"

Finally, a voice came through, softly saying, "Beta…"

In an instant, all of Rachit's emotions spilled out as a single, glistening tear rolled down his cheek. With a trembling voice, he managed to say, "Mmmm… Maa…?"

On the other end, the voice responded with warmth and excitement, "Happy Birthday, Beta!"

As soon as Rachit realized that it was his mother calling him, a wave of relief washed over him, and he couldn't hold back his tears any longer. Overwhelmed with joy, he began to cry, feeling the love and connection he had longed for.

Rachit clutched his phone tightly, tears cascading down his cheeks like a sudden rainstorm. The sound of his sobs reached Tara, his mother, and a wave of concern washed over her. Despite their frequent conversations since his move to Norway, she had never encountered this level of distress in her son before.

"Beta, what happened? Rachit, what's wrong? Why are you crying so much? Oh God, why is this boy doing this?" she questioned, her voice laced with worry.

Taking a moment to gather himself, Rachit took a deep breath and replied, "Maa, wait, I'll video call you, just give me 2 minutes."

With a flicker of excitement igniting within him, he ended the call and rushed to grab his laptop, his hands trembling with anticipation like a child on the brink of a surprise. As he hastily set up the video call, the familiar face of his mother appeared on the screen almost instantly. A surge of joy filled Rachit as he reached out, almost instinctively, as if he could bridge the distance between them by touching her face through the laptop.

"Why were you crying so much?" she asked, concern etched across her features.

Rachit, dabbing at his tears, confessed, "Maa, I was missing you a lot. This is my first birthday without you, and you didn't even call me to wish me."

His mother's expression softened, a shadow of sadness crossing her face as she responded, "You couldn't make a single call to me? You knew that I still can't understand the time difference between us, wondering what time it is for you and what time it is for me. It's so frustrating!"

Then Rachit apologized to his mom, saying, "Sorry Mom, from now on I'll call you immediately and I won't get angry with you."

His mom also started to apologize, "Forgive me too, I woke you up in the middle of the night and wished you a late birthday. After you left, the house felt very quiet, and I ended up spending a lot of time on the remaining work. That's why I was a bit late today. But I remembered, just took a little while to wish you."

Hearing this, Rachit smiled and said, "It's okay, Mom, you are forgiven by your son."

Saying this, both of them started laughing loudly. Then Rachit asked, "But Mom, which number did you call from? This number is different."

Tara explained, "Yes, my old SIM wasn't getting any network, and I had to call you today. Porting the SIM takes about two days, so I got a new SIM and called you immediately."

While talking, Rachit noticed that his mom wasn't alone at home; someone else was there too. He asked his mom, "Mom, is there anyone else at home besides you?" Just then, someone peeked in from the side, and Rachit saw that it was his friend Yash!

Rachit exclaimed joyfully, "Hey, you're here?!!"

Yash replied, "Yeah, where else would I be on your birthday?"

Rachit continued, "Dude, you could have at least called me to wish me a happy birthday, but you didn't!"

Yash explained, "It was all Auntie's plan. She insisted that we both wish you together, so I didn't message you. Wait a second."

Yash went inside and returned with a delicious-looking cake, saying, "Look at how much effort we put into this for you, and you were getting so angry with us!"

Rachit quickly apologized, "Sorry, sorry! Please forgive me, I'll even hold my ears!"

Then Tara chimed in, "Beta, why don't you also bring some cake or something similar? We can cut the cake here, and you can cut yours over there."

Rachit responded, "Mom, that's a good idea, but I need to see what we have. Wait a minute, I'll check in the kitchen."

Rachit went into the kitchen and started checking the items he had brought from the supermarket. Among the groceries, he found a packet of bread and a jar of chocolate spread in the fridge. Quickly, he took out three slices of bread and spread the chocolate between them, creating a small makeshift cake. Now, he began searching for candles.

Unfortunately, he couldn't find any birthday candles, but he did discover a large candle that belonged to his roommate, who had gone back to his hometown for the winter holidays. Rachit grabbed the big candle and stuck it into the cake.

When he joined the video call, Tara exclaimed, "What is this, Rachit? Such a big candle!"

Rachit replied, "Mom, it's what I found, and it's enough!"

Tara responded, "Alright, fine."

Then, Tara and Yash lit the candle in Mumbai, while Rachit lit his candle at the same time. As soon as the candles were lit, Tara and Yash began singing the "Happy Birthday" song, creating a joyful atmosphere despite the distance.

Yash and Tara sang together, "Happy Birthday to you! Happy Birthday dear Rachit! Happy Birthday to you!"

As they sang, Yash pulled out a hair dryer from behind him, with Rachit's photo taped to it. Seeing this, Rachit couldn't help but laugh.

Just as he was about to blow out the candles, there was a sudden knock at the door. Rachit turned his attention towards the door, puzzled about who could be visiting at such a late hour. He knew that the people in the building rarely disturbed anyone, and without keys, no one could enter the building. This thought made him a bit anxious as he wondered what was happening.

Tara and Yash noticed the fear on Rachit's face and asked, "What's wrong, Rachit?"

He replied, "I don't know, Mom. Who could be knocking at the door at this hour? This has never happened before."

Tara suggested, "Maybe your roommate Ryan has come back."

Rachit shook his head, saying, "No, Mom, he can't be back this early."

Just then, there was another knock at the door, and Rachit's anxiety grew as he wondered who it could be. He turned to Tara and Yash, saying, "Wait, I'll check."

Tara cautioned him, "Be careful, son."

Overcome with fear, Rachit grabbed Ryan's baseball bat, which was kept under the bed, and cautiously approached the door. He called out, "Who is it? Who's out there?"

But there was no response. The person outside continued to knock repeatedly, louder and more insistently. In a state of panic, Rachit shouted, "Go away, or I'll call the police! I have a weapon!" At that moment, the knocking abruptly stopped. Rachit's mind raced with questions, urging him to figure out who could be outside at this late hour, compelling him to open the door.

Rachit opened the door cautiously, but the entire lobby was suddenly silent, as if no one was in the building. Rachit's floor resembled a long lobby, with other flats on the left side and a window for ventilation, while the right side had stairs. When Rachit went to close his door, he noticed a small box sitting at the bottom of his door. His heart started racing as he thought, "Who left this box here at this hour?"

He walked over to the stairs to check If someone might have hidden something on the upper or lower floors. When he reached the stairs, he called out, "Is anyone here? Look, if someone is playing a prank, I'm really not in the mood for such a scary joke. I'm saying this one last time, if anyone is here, show yourself!"

After a moment of waiting, there was no sound coming from anywhere. Feeling uneasy, Rachit decided he should go back to his apartment because that would be the safest option. Just as he turned from the stairs toward his door, he saw that the box lying on the floor had disappeared.

Seeing this made Rachit feel a chill run down his spine, and he quickly rushed back into his apartment. Rachit was consumed with worry, wondering if someone might have entered his home. Thinking this, he turned on all the lights and began to search every corner of his apartment, checking the kitchen, the wardrobe, and even looking under the bed shared with Ryan. After thoroughly checking, he found no one inside, and a small sigh of relief escaped him.

He then turned off the lights and sat down in

front of his laptop, only to discover that the video call had been disconnected. He tried to call his mother again, but the call didn't go through. Frustrated, he attempted to make a normal call from his phone, yet he still couldn't reach her. Then it dawned on him that his mother mentioned there were network issues in their area. He decided to wait until tomorrow to talk to her. As he closed his laptop and placed it back on his study table, he could hardly believe his eyes when he saw the box that had been outside his door now sitting on his table.

This shock transformed the moment of joy he felt at the thought of speaking to his mother into one of sheer terror, all because of that mysterious box. He was left wondering how the box made its way inside on its own. The unsettling thought lingered in his mind, amplifying his fear and confusion.

Fig 2. In the dead of night, Rachit discovered an isolated box at his doorstep. Gripped by fear, he clutched a bat for safety.

3.

Mystery
And
Mayhem

Suddenly, a mysterious box appeared on Rachit's study table, seemingly out of nowhere. There was no one around at the time, yet the box sat there as if it had materialized on its own. A chilling thought crept into Rachit's mind—could this be the work of that shadowy, human-like figure he had glimpsed before?

An unsettling fear gripped him, making his heart pound. Determined to shake off his growing unease, he searched every corner of his flat, inspecting every room with anxious eyes. But no matter how thoroughly he looked, he found no trace of another presence—not a single sound, not the faintest sign that anyone had been there. The eerie silence only deepened his dread, leaving him with more questions than answers.

Rachit slowly walked back to his study table and sank into his chair, his mind racing with unanswered questions. His eyes remained fixed on the mysterious box as he tried to make sense of its sudden appearance.

"Who could have left it here? And why?" he wondered. "If this is some kind of prank, then who is behind it?"

He studied the box carefully. It was a perfect square, its edges sharp and precise, as if crafted with meticulous precision. But what unsettled him the most was its colour—a deep, matte black so intense that it seemed to swallow the light around it. There were no markings, no symbols, no name—nothing to hint at its origin. It sat there in eerie silence, offering no clues, yet demanding his attention. The more Rachit stared at it, the more it seemed like an enigma, something beyond the ordinary, something that shouldn't be there.

A single thought kept running through Rachit's mind—

"What could have compelled someone to give me this gift in the middle of the night?"

Everything that had happened since that mysterious knock on the door felt far from normal. There was an eerie strangeness to it all that he couldn't ignore.

Determined to push past his fear, he steeled himself. "I have to open the box, no matter what happens. I can't keep overthinking and letting fear control me."

With that, he picked up the box, its smooth, matte-black surface absorbing the dim light of the room. Taking a deep breath, he carefully lifted the lid.

Inside, resting in the centre, was a ring.

The ring had a dark greyish hue, but as Rachit examined it more closely, he immediately realized it was no ordinary piece of jewellery. He placed the box back on his study table and held the ring in his hand, inspecting its structure.

It wasn't a simple, single-band ring like those commonly found in stores. Instead, it had an intricate design—two layers stacked atop each other. The upper layer, in particular, felt slightly loose, as if it wasn't fixed in place.

As he observed further, he noticed something even more unusual—the upper layer appeared to be rotatable.

Though he hadn't tried turning it yet, the realization sent a fresh wave of curiosity through him. Then, something else caught his attention. There were markings on the ring, subtle engravings along its surface. His eyes narrowed as he tried to decipher them under the dim glow of his study lamp, but the light wasn't bright enough. He needed a clearer view.

It was late at night, and the dim glow of the study lamp wasn't enough for Rachit to clearly see the engravings on the ring. Realizing this, he walked to the hall and switched on the main light. Under the brighter illumination, the details on the ring became clearer.

Four distinct symbols were etched at equal distances along the upper layer of the ring. As he studied them closely, he slowly began to grasp their meaning—they represented the four basic elements: Fire, Water, Earth, and Air.

The Fire and Water symbols were the easiest to recognize. Fire was depicted as a small, flickering flame, while Water was represented by a simple yet elegant droplet. However, the other two symbols weren't as immediately obvious.

Curious, Rachit turned to his laptop and began researching. To his surprise, while the exact designs weren't an exact match, he found similar symbols scattered across various ancient sculptures and texts. These four elements weren't just symbols—they had existed across civilizations, religions, and mythologies for centuries, woven into the very fabric of history.

Just as he was piecing everything together, his eyes drifted back to the box. That's when he noticed something strange.

Lying exactly where the ring had been just moments ago was a white card.

Rachit's heart skipped a beat. He was absolutely certain — when he had picked up the ring, the box had been empty. There had been no card inside.

So where had it come from? How had it appeared out of nowhere?

His hands trembled slightly as he reached for the card. It was completely blank on one side, stark white and unmarked. But when he flipped it over, bold letters stared back at him:

"HAPPY BIRTHDAY, It's Time….!"

Rachit sat back down at his study table, his fingers absentmindedly tracing the edges of the white card. His eyes lingered on the words written in bold —

"It's Time."

The phrase refused to leave his mind, gnawing at him with an unsettling persistence. Time for what? Was something about to happen? The very thought scared him.

Trying to calm himself, he considered a more rational explanation. Could this be a surprise planned by Mom? Maybe she had arranged for this ring as a birthday gift. That would explain everything, wouldn't it?

But no matter how much he tried to reassure himself, his mind kept circling back to the same haunting question — how did the box get inside in the first place? That was the only thing he couldn't reason away. Everything else he could dismiss, but this? It was impossible to ignore.

A sudden urgency gripped him. If this was a birthday surprise, his mom would surely know something about it. Without wasting another second, he grabbed his phone and dialled her number, hoping for an answer that would put his mind at ease.

"The number you are trying to reach is currently out of network coverage."

The automated message made his stomach twist in discomfort. His mother's phone was unreachable. That was unusual. Frowning, he tried again — same result.

His next instinct was to call Yash, his closest friend. If anyone knew about a birthday plan, it would be him. Yash had been involved in every surprise his mom had planned in the past. But when Rachit dialed his number, the response was eerily the same.

Frustrated and feeling trapped, he hurled his phone onto the desk in disbelief before mustering the courage to open his door, hoping to find solace or answers outside.

As he stepped into the empty lobby, the stillness of the surroundings only heightened his sense of isolation and dread. The once-familiar spaces now seemed hauntingly empty, amplifying the nightmarish quality of the situation. Rachit's quest for clarity and reassurance had led him to a place where every corner seemed to hold a mystery, leaving him to grapple with the unknown alone.

"The number you are trying to reach is currently out of network coverage."

Rachit's fingers tightened around his phone. Something didn't feel right.

A quick glance at his own phone's status bar confirmed that he had full network coverage. His calls should have gone through. There was no reason why both his mom and Yash would be out of reach at the same time. A strange unease settled in his chest.

Who else could he call at this hour? He didn't have many close contacts, and certainly no one he could rely on to rush to his house in the middle of the night. For the first time that night, Rachit felt truly alone.

Rachit took a deep breath and shook his head.

"Enough of this. I'm overthinking. Let's just wear the ring and see what happens."

Determined to put his doubts aside, he slid the ring onto his finger.

To his surprise, it fit perfectly — as if it had been made just for him. There was no looseness, no tightness. It settled onto his finger with an almost unnatural precision.

Curious, he ran his thumb over the ring's surface, trying to get a feel for its texture. The moment his thumb brushed against the upper layer, something unexpected happened. The ring's top layer shifted ever so slightly, rotating just a fraction before stopping.

A sound of "Click" came from the ring.

Rachit's breath caught in his throat. For a brief moment, fear gripped him. He froze, half expecting something strange to happen.

But nothing did. The room remained silent. Everything was exactly as it had been before. Still, his heart pounded in his chest.

Seeking solace in the mundane, Rachit tried to calm his nerves and proceeded with his daily routine, albeit with the lingering trauma weighing heavily on his mind. Returning to his desk, he indulged in a bite of the cake (stack of bread) left there.

Unfortunately, a chunk of bread became lodged in his throat, prompting him to rush to the kitchen for water, carrying the bottle back with him. Upon his return, as he placed the bottle on the desk, he was astonished to find that the cake (stack of bread) had metamorphosed into a pastry, with a subtle slice missing from one end, indicating that someone had taken a portion.

Rachit was taken aback by this inexplicable transformation, realizing that the amount missing from the pastry precisely matched the portion of bread he had consumed earlier. The inexplicable events unfolding before him only added to the mystique and uncertainty shrouding his reality.

In that state of uncertainty, he began to realize that the ring was the key to all these strange happenings. He turned the ring once more, and the familiar "click" sound echoed through the air.

As he touched the bottle, its appearance changed in the blink of an eye. He decided to rotate the ring again, this time with more force, causing the "click" sound to occur twice. When he touched the bottle once more, he observed it undergoing two transformations before settling on the second one.

Despite the changes in its physical form, the object's fundamental purpose remained unchanged. The mysterious ability of the ring to alter the appearance of objects without altering their essence added a new layer of complexity to his bewildering experience.

As he continued to rotate the ring and experiment with different objects, their appearances kept changing, adding an element of enjoyment to his discovery. However, his amusement turned to concern as he attempted to remove the ring from his finger, only to find it jammed in place.

Despite applying more force and even resorting to using soap to ease its removal, the ring stubbornly refused to budge. But in his haste, he accidentally twisted the upper layer of the ring too forcefully. A strange sensation followed — it was as if the ring had locked itself in place. No matter how much he tried, it wouldn't budge.

As he watched closely, his heart pounded. The ring's colour was changing, shifting from a dull grey to an off-white marble-like texture. His hands trembled. The more the upper layer spun, the faster it moved, heating up unnaturally. Before he could process what was happening, sharp spikes emerged from the inner band, piercing deep into his fingers.

A sharp, searing pain shot through his hand. Blood trickled from the wounds, staining the sink. His breath quickened. Desperate, he splashed cold water over his hand, hoping to ease the pain. But something was wrong—terribly wrong. His vision blurred, his head grew dizzy, and the room around him twisted unnaturally, as if reality itself were warping.

And then, in the mirror—he saw it.

At first, he thought it was just his reflection. But the figure staring back wasn't merely mimicking his actions. It was him—yet something was off. The same ring adorned its hand, its movements eerily synchronized. But the reflection's eyes held something sinister, something beyond his understanding.

Panic surged through him. He grabbed a towel and wrapped it around his bleeding fingers, stumbling towards his phone to call for help. But before he could reach it, something hard struck his foot. He tripped.

A dull thud echoed as he hit the floor, his head smacking against the cold tiles. A sharp pain throbbed in his skull, but he forced himself to move,

pushing up onto his knees. That's when he felt it —
his entire flat was trembling. The furniture, the walls,
the very air around him vibrated violently, as though
the whole world was unravelling.

He couldn't take it anymore. A terrified
scream escaped his lips, but before the sound could
fully leave his throat — he vanished.

Silence.

The vibrations ceased. The walls stood still.
The air was quiet, save for the faint whisper of the
wind creeping through the cracks of the apartment.
Rachit was gone. And all that remained was an eerie,
hollow stillness.

Fig 3. Ring's Portrait

4.

Astral

Destiny

Rachit slowly opened his eyes, only to be met with an unbelievable sight — he was floating in the vast expanse of space, staring down at Earth in all its breath-taking glory. His mind refused to accept the reality before him. Was he really seeing the planet from space? How was that even possible?

Doubt gripped him as he raised a trembling hand and slapped himself — once, twice — trying to wake up from what he assumed was a dream. But the cold emptiness around him felt too real. Panic began to creep in. He wasn't wearing a spacesuit, yet he was alive. How?

As the moments passed, he realized with growing dread that he was slowly drifting farther away from Earth. He flailed his arms, kicked his legs, desperately trying to propel himself back toward the planet, but it was futile. The vast, merciless void had claimed him, pulling him deeper into the unknown.

Was this fate? Or a cruel trick of the universe? Either way, there was no turning back.

One by one, Rachit drifted past the planets of the Solar System, moving steadily toward the vast, uncharted depths of outer space. He had no control over his movement — it was as if some unseen force was pulling him along an invisible path.

As soon as he crossed the boundary of the Solar System, he suddenly came to a halt. Confusion gripped him. Why had he stopped? Until now, everything that had happened was beyond his control, and this was no different. Then, he noticed something strange. The very fabric of space in front of him seemed to be collapsing inward, drawing closer to him, while behind him, it felt as if an immense force was pressing from all sides. It was as though space itself was compressing around him, distorting distances in a way that defied logic.

And then, without warning, he began to move again. At first, his speed was barely noticeable, but the space around him seemed to rush past at an impossible pace. It was as if someone had deliberately created a wormhole just for him, or perhaps he had stumbled into a region of warped space-time. The very structure of space appeared to bend and ripple around him, stretching and curving in ways he could hardly comprehend.

Then his velocity began to increase — gradually at first, then exponentially. Soon, he was accelerating beyond anything he could endure. Galaxies, stars, and planets flashed past him in a blur, moving at speeds far beyond the limits of light itself. The sheer force of his acceleration became unbearable, pressing against him with an overwhelming intensity.

At last, the motion became so rapid that he could no longer perceive anything around him—just streaks of light, an endless cascade of luminous trails. His mind, unable to process the enormity of what was happening, began slipping into an altered state. And in that strange, unfathomable mind-space, new visions began to appear—images, sensations, fragments of something beyond human understanding.

Rachit found himself witnessing a scene entirely removed from the chaos of space. It was as if his consciousness had been transported into a memory—one not his own, yet strangely familiar.

Before him, a young woman, no older than 24, lay asleep in her bedroom. The soft glow of morning light filtered through the curtains, casting a warm hue over the room. Suddenly, a loud knock on the door shattered the quiet. A voice—gentle yet urgent—called from the other side.

"Tara, wake up! You have to leave for the concert today. Hurry up, or you'll be late—it won't be good for you if you miss it!"

The name sent a jolt through Rachit. This wasn't just any girl. This was his mother, Tara. And what he was seeing—this wasn't reality. It was a flashback, a glimpse into her past.

Tara's eyes fluttered open, and the moment realization struck, she leaped out of bed. "Yes, Mom! I'm coming…!" she called out, her voice filled with excitement.

With hurried steps, she got ready—eating breakfast quickly, styling her hair just right, and selecting the perfect outfit. Before stepping out, she paused for a moment in front of the mirror, tilting her head slightly as she admired her reflection. A playful smile touched her lips.

"I hope no one casts an evil eye on me today," she mused, adjusting her hair one last time before grabbing her bag.

Without wasting another second, she rushed outside, flagged down a rickshaw, and set off.

The streets of Mumbai were abuzz with anticipation. Today was no ordinary day—it was the day M. Jackson was performing in the city for the very first time. A historic event. A once-in-a-lifetime experience. As Tara made her way to the concert venue, she met up with her friends, their energy infectious as they chattered excitedly about the night ahead.

When they arrived, the sight before them was overwhelming. The crowd was unlike anything Mumbai had ever seen before—an ocean of fans, thousands upon thousands, all gathered for a glimpse of the King of Pop. The atmosphere pulsed with electricity, a mixture of anticipation, euphoria, and the sheer magic of the moment.

Rachit, watching this unfold like a silent observer trapped in time, felt his heart tighten. He was witnessing a part of his mother's life—a past he had never known, a moment she had once lived, now playing before his eyes like an old film reel. And he had no idea why.

The concert had begun, and the atmosphere was electric. The crowd swayed and sang in unison, completely immersed in the magic of the moment. Tara, too, was lost in pure euphoria—after all, she was finally seeing the man she had idolized for years. M. Jackson was right there, performing before her eyes. It felt surreal.

Time slipped away unnoticed, swept away by the music and the energy of the night. No one cared about anything else in that moment.

After a while, Tara turned to her friends and said, "Wait here, I'll be right back. I need to get some water."

She carefully navigated through the densely packed crowd, making her way toward a nearby stall. When she arrived, she was disappointed to learn that all the water bottles had been sold out. Even the cold drinks were gone — there was nothing left to quench her thirst. With a sigh, she turned back, ready to re-join her friends, though the dryness in her throat made her steps feel heavier.

Just then, a voice called out from behind her.

"Hello! Blue T-shirt girl!"

Tara froze mid-step. She was wearing a blue T-shirt. Was someone calling her? She turned around, her eyes searching for the source of the voice.

Walking toward her was a young man — tall, well-built, and undeniably handsome. His features were striking, his presence effortlessly commanding. For a brief moment, Tara felt as if the world around her had blurred, and she completely lost track of reality.

The young man approached her, a kind smile on his face. "Hi, I saw you asking for water at the stall. I know they ran out, but if you don't mind sharing, I have a full bottle with me."

Tara didn't respond — she was still caught in the daze of his unexpected presence. The boy chuckled softly, waving a hand in front of her face. "Hello? Are you listening?"

Snapping back to reality, she quickly composed herself. "Oh! Sorry, what were you saying? I didn't hear you properly. The music is really loud."

He smiled again, shaking his head slightly. "I was saying, I have a full bottle of water. Since I'm here alone, I don't mind sharing. If you'd like some, you're welcome to it."

Tara hesitated for only a second before he extended the bottle toward her. The thirst was unbearable, and right now, this was exactly what she needed. She took it gratefully and drank in hurried gulps, the cool liquid soothing her parched throat instantly.

Handing the bottle back, she let out a satisfied sigh. "That was a lifesaver. Thank you."

The boy took the bottle back with an amused expression. "You drank quite a bit, you know? Guess I'll have to manage with whatever's left." He smirked and turned to leave.

Before she could think, Tara called out, "Hey, wait!"

He turned back, raising an eyebrow.

"You said you're here alone, right? Would you like to join me and my friends?"

His face lit up. "Sure, why not? By the way, my name's Anant. And yours?"

Tara extended her hand with a smile. "I'm Tara."

And just like that, they spent the rest of the concert together, sharing laughter, music, and moments that felt effortless and warm. The connection between them was instant, and by the time the night ended, they had become fast friends.

As they stepped out of the concert venue, Anant hesitated before speaking. "Hey, would it be alright if I got your number?"

At that time, personal phones weren't common, but Tara was lucky — she had a telephone in her room. She nodded and shared her number with him.

"Got it," Anant said with a grin. "I'll call you."

Tara smiled back. "I hope you do."

And with that, they parted ways, the echoes of the concert still ringing in the night air, marking the beginning of something neither of them had expected.

Days passed after the concert, but Anant had yet to call. Tara found herself glancing at the telephone more often than she cared to admit, hoping to hear from him. She told herself not to overthink it—perhaps he was busy, or maybe he had forgotten. But deep down, a part of her wanted him to remember, to reach out.

Then, just as she was lost in these thoughts, the phone rang.

Her heart skipped a beat. Without wasting a second, she grabbed the receiver and held it to her ear—but she didn't speak. She waited, listening for any sign of who was on the other end.

For a few moments, there was only silence. Then, just as she opened her mouth to say something, a voice echoed at the exact same moment—

"Hello!"

They had spoken in unison. And the unexpected timing made both of them burst into laughter.

From that moment on, the conversation flowed naturally. They talked about everything and nothing, sharing stories, exchanging little details about their lives.

It was during one of these conversations that Tara learned Anant was originally from Kashmir. "I'm only in Mumbai for a few months," he told her.

"Work brought me here. It's different from home, but I like it."

Something about the way he spoke — calm, thoughtful — made Tara want to keep listening. And so, night after night, their calls became longer.

Soon, it became a routine. Every evening, after the day had settled, their voices would find each other through the crackling telephone line. Their conversations stretched late into the night, filled with laughter, stories, and moments of quiet understanding.

Neither of them had planned for this, but somehow, it felt like the most natural thing in the world.

Over time, their interactions deepened, nurturing the growth of a profound friendship. They revelled in each other's presence, sharing moments at cozy cafes, leisurely hangouts, movie outings, and delightful dinners. Eventually, the realization dawned upon them — they had fallen deeply in love. Their connection thrived as they embraced life together, savouring each moment and fortifying their bond.

Tara wanted Anant to be a part of her world, to be accepted by the people who mattered most to her. So, one evening, she invited him over for dinner, hoping to introduce him to her parents. She wanted them to see what she saw in him—to understand why he was special.

Anant arrived, polite and respectful, making every effort to leave a good impression. But as the evening unfolded, it became clear that Tara's parents were unimpressed. They watched him with wary eyes, their silence heavy with unspoken judgment. And when dinner was over, her father finally spoke.

"You may finish your meal," he said, his voice firm and unwavering, "but after tonight, we don't want you meeting our daughter again."

Anant, though visibly hurt, didn't argue. He simply nodded, thanked them for their hospitality, and left.

As soon as the door closed behind him, the house erupted into chaos.

"Dad, please!" Tara pleaded, her voice trembling with frustration. "I like him—no, I love him! Why are you doing this?"

Her father's expression hardened. "Because we don't even know him properly, Tara. And do you honestly believe everything he's told you about his family? He's from Kashmir—what if he's hiding something? What if he isn't who he says he is?"

His words stung, laced with distrust and prejudice. Tara couldn't believe what she was hearing. Without another word, she turned away and stormed into her room, slamming the door behind her.

Later that night, she called Anant. Her voice was quiet but determined.

"Let's run away."

Anant hesitated. "Tara—"

"They'll never accept us," she cut him off. "No matter how hard I try, they'll never change their minds. If we want to be together, we have to leave."

There was silence on the other end of the line, but Tara knew he was listening. Finally, he exhaled. "Alright," he said. "If this is what you want, we'll do it together."

And so, one fateful night, Tara left her home behind. She didn't look back.

Since Anant still had time before he had to return to Kashmir, they found a small place to rent in Mumbai, a temporary refuge where they could be together, away from prying eyes and judgmental voices.

One evening, as they sat together in their modest new home, Tara reached for Anant's hand.

"Once we get to Kashmir," she whispered, her eyes filled with hope, "we'll get married."

Months later, while living with Anant, Tara suddenly collapsed, sending Anant into a panic. Hastily, he whisked her to the hospital, where a flurry of medical assessments commenced. Anxiously awaiting news in the hospital's lobby, his thoughts raced. Soon, the doctors returned with a startling revelation—Tara, still unconscious, was confirmed to be carrying a child.

Overwhelmed and perspiring with disbelief, Anant stuttered, seeking confirmation, "Are you certain?"

The doctors' affirmative response left him stunned. With resolve, he instructed, "Very well, prepare the necessary documents. I will retrieve cash from the ATM downstairs."

As hours slipped by, there was no trace of him. Tara, now conscious and relieved, was overjoyed upon hearing the news of her pregnancy. However, her elation was short-lived. The doctors, with sombre expressions, inquired about her husband.

Tara clarified, "He's not my husband; we are in a living relationship."

The doctors gravely informed her, "Regrettably, he has not returned from the ATM visit in front of the hospital. It has been 5-6 hours, and there is no sign of his return."

This revelation struck Tara deeply. Despite their strong bond, the circumstances painted a bleak picture, hinting at a possible abandonment due to the pregnancy. The weight of this realization shattered her, yet she found strength in her resolve to raise the child alone. Despite the heartache, she persisted in trying to reach him, clinging to hope that he would come back one day, bringing with him answers to the questions that now loomed large in her heart.

As the baby's arrival drew near, Tara's routine day took a sudden turn. On her way back from work, she was seized by intense labour pains, causing her to writhe in agony. Thankfully, kind souls around her swiftly came to her aid, escorting her to the hospital.

In the delivery room, amidst the chaos of preparations for surgery, Tara's pain intensified, echoing through the room. Her cries filled the air as she lay on the bed, grappling with the waves of pain. In a moment etched in time, as Tara gazed upwards in distress, a breath-taking sight unfolded before her eyes—a glimpse of the universe painted on the ceiling, a surreal spectacle that momentarily captivated her, even amidst the throes of pain.

In the blink of an eye, Rachit made his entrance into the world, ushering in a sense of normalcy. Overwhelmed, Tara succumbed to unconsciousness in the wake of the whirlwind of emotions and physical strain. Upon regaining consciousness, her mind revisited the fleeting vision of the universe above, dismissing it as a mere trick of pain-induced illusions.

Discharged from the hospital after a few days, Tara returned home with Rachit cradled in her arms. Tears of joy cascaded down her cheeks as she held her new-born son, her heart brimming with happiness and gratitude for the precious gift of motherhood.

As the sun began to set on that tranquil Sunday evening, Tara and Rachit inhabited their cozy home with a modest backyard adorned with delicate tufts of grass. Rachit's laughter danced through the air as he played in the yard, while Tara, occupied with preparing dinner, glanced out the kitchen window, ensuring his safety in the fading light.

Upon stepping outside to call Rachit in for dinner, Tara was met with a peculiar sight. Rachit stood beneath the night sky, his small hand reaching towards the stars above, seemingly engaged in a silent conversation with the celestial bodies. Perplexed yet intrigued, Tara approached him, only to find that Rachit persisted in his ethereal interaction with the night sky.

In a moment of astonishment, Rachit made a swift motion, and a shooting star streaked across the heavens, leaving Tara in a state of wonder and disbelief. Reacting swiftly to the magical encounter, Tara gently lifted Rachit into her arms and hastened inside, her mind abuzz with the extraordinary connection between her son and the vast expanse above. The incident left Tara pondering the inexplicable bond between Rachit and the cosmic realm, a bond that defied the confines of the ordinary and hinted at a world of enchantment and mystery just beyond their reach.

As the years passed by, Rachit grew into an 8-year-old with a mischievous and lively spirit, often testing Tara's patience as she managed the household. Despite their modest financial situation, Tara ensured they had enough to meet their basic needs, providing for Rachit's upbringing with care and dedication.

One eventful day, after returning from school, Rachit's mischievous antics escalated, leading to a moment of frustration where Tara, overwhelmed, resorted to a slap in response to his persistent annoyance. Tears welled up in Rachit's eyes as he retreated to his room, his emotions swirling in a tumultuous storm of anger and sadness.

Inside his room, Rachit's cries transformed into anguished shouts, echoing through the house with an intensity that unsettled Tara. Alarmed by the escalating situation, Tara rushed to his side, witnessing his frantic movements and distressed state. In a moment of desperation and concern, she enveloped him in a tight embrace, trying to soothe his turmoil.

In that charged moment, as Rachit gazed upwards, his eyes seemed to hold the entire universe within them, evoking a profound sense of déjà vu within Tara. Memories flooded back to her of a similar cosmic encounter during Rachit's birth, where the universe seemed to reveal itself on the hospital room ceiling.

Sweating with anxiety and confusion, Tara searched the ceiling for answers, only to find emptiness, leaving her grappling with her own thoughts and emotions in the face of this inexplicable and unsettling experience.

In a sudden and bewildering turn of events, Rachit found himself jolted from his reality into the vast expanse of outer space. As he traversed this cosmic journey, his senses were overwhelmed by the sight of two distinct energy forms, resembling human figures, embracing each other.

A mesmerizing transformation unfolded before his eyes as these energies merged, giving birth to a minuscule white circle that rapidly expanded, engulfing his surroundings in a brilliant white light. Amidst this ethereal transition, Rachit discovered himself suspended in weightlessness, a solitary figure in the cosmic void.

His solitude was soon interrupted by the arrival of another entity, materializing in a similar teleportation fashion. Struggling to comprehend this surreal experience, Rachit's contemplation was abruptly interrupted by the sudden appearance of a middle-aged man clad.

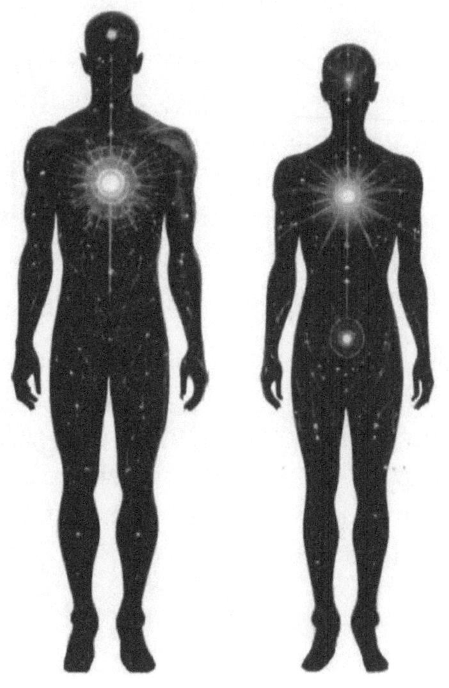

Fig 4. The human forms that rachit saw in his vision.

5.

Temporal Echoes: The Rings Of Destiny

Rachit was traveling at the speed of light when, all of a sudden, he came to an abrupt halt. It was as if he was floating, weightless, without any sense of gravity. As he looked around, he found himself surrounded by an endless white void—no sky above, no ground beneath, and no familiar universe filled with planets and stars. There was nothing but an infinite expanse of white in every direction.

Due to the absence of gravity, he spun uncontrollably, unable to find stability. A wave of panic surged through him as he tried to scream, but no sound escaped his throat. It was as if his voice had been swallowed by the void itself. The suffocating silence and weightlessness made him feel as though he was on the brink of death.

With great effort, Rachit managed to steady himself, his eyes scanning the endless whiteness for anything—any sign of life, any clue about where he was. And then, at a distance, he spotted something— someone. A figure, human-like in shape, was approaching. But the way it arrived was unnatural. It seemed as though a force of dark light had violently pushed the being forward, as if even gravity itself resisted its presence.

As the figure drifted closer, it struggled against the same weightlessness that plagued Rachit.

He could now make out long, flowing hair and delicate features—it was a woman. Their eyes met, and for a brief moment, a glimmer of hope flickered within Rachit. Perhaps she held the answers he so desperately sought.

Determined to reach her, he fought against the void, flailing his limbs in an attempt to propel himself forward. It felt like he was swimming through an invisible ocean, each movement an exhausting battle. But as he drew closer, he noticed something strange—the woman was trying to get away from him. She struggled just as he did, moving in the opposite direction, as if she feared him.

As Rachit struggled against the weightlessness, a sudden, deafening sound tore through the void, so powerful that it felt as if his eardrums would burst. The sheer intensity of the sound sent a wave of unbearable pain crashing through his skull. Every nerve in his body vibrated violently, and he could feel the sound waves rattling his very bones.

Amidst the agony, he noticed something— this sound wasn't coming from everywhere; it had a source. Squinting through the distortion, he forced himself to look in the direction of the noise. Far, far in the distance, he could barely make out a small figure. But the immense sound made it nearly impossible to see clearly. The figure flickered erratically, as if its presence was unstable, distorted by the very vibrations shaking the void.

His gaze instinctively darted back t" the girl. She, too, writhed in pain, clutching her head just as he was. Her face contorted in agony, mirroring his own suffering. Before he could process anything further, a deep, commanding voice boomed through the void, vibrating with a heavy bass that resonated in his chest.

"CALM DOWN."

The words rang out in pure, radiant white, cutting through the chaos. And then, just like that, the unbearable noise ceased. A heavy silence settled over the void, and Rachit gasped for air, finally feeling some relief.

As he steadied himself, he noticed something strange. The distant figure—the one that had been the source of the sound—was now clearly visible. It was a man, seated with his arms spread wide, as if he had just unleashed that overwhelming force. Before Rachit could react, a sudden, invisible force yanked him forward. He barely had time to register what was happening before both he and the girl were being pulled toward the man, like iron drawn to a magnet.

In the blink of an eye, they were face to face.

Now, standing directly before him, Rachit could see them both clearly. The girl looked entirely human—beautiful, delicate, and innocent, though her face still bore traces of the pain she had just endured. Opposite her stood the man who had pulled them in. He appeared middle-aged, dressed in an immaculate black three-piece suit that stood in stark contrast to the pure white void surrounding them. His salt-and-pepper hair, a mix of black and white strands, gave him a distinguished yet slightly ominous appearance.

Rachit opened his mouth to speak, but no words came out. Panic flickered across his face as he tried again—still nothing. The girl beside him also attempted to say something, but like him, she was rendered completely mute.

The suited man, noticing their frustration, let out a small chuckle. And strangely enough, his laughter rang out perfectly clear, unaffected by whatever force had stolen their voices

With an air of authority, the suited man introduced himself. "My name is Vedan, the creator of the universe," he declared. His presence was both imposing and reassuring, and he continued, "I understand that you both have many questions. But fear not; I will answer every single one." He turned to Rachit and Ciona, making the introductions with a gentle nod. "Rachit, this is Ciona. And Ciona, meet Rachit."

As he spoke, Rachit felt a strange comfort in the connection they were forming. "I am able to converse with you using my telepathic powers," Vedan explained. "The reason for this method is that we are currently in a place known as the void, a complete vacuum where not a single matter exists." Vedan's voice softened as he continued, "Now, let me bestow my powers upon you both, so that you may navigate this void with ease." With that, an ethereal energy began to envelop Rachit and Ciona, a shimmering light that promised the strength they needed to endure the emptiness surrounding them.

Now Rachit and Ciona could feel the transition happening within them. In the meantime, they had both gained powers like Vedan, but they were still unaware of how to use them. Vedan began to speak as soon as they were able to communicate with him. Just as he was about to share his thoughts, Rachit interrupted, his eyes drawn to the ring on Ciona's hand.

"Ciona, can you show me your hand?" he asked, intrigued.

As she revealed it, he examined the ring closely. Both rings were completely identical, featuring the same intricate structure and symbols. The only difference was that their ring had once been a dark greyish colour, but now transformed to a marble white, likely due to the ring's earlier rotation. Ciona nodded in agreement with Rachit's observations. Before they could delve deeper into their discoveries, Vedan interjected.

"I was the one who sent these rings to you, in order to bring you to the void."

Rachit spoke hastily, frustration evident in his tone. "Was it necessary to send it on my birthday and ruin it…?!"

Ciona quickly added, "I also received the ring on my birthday, and it caused havoc!"

Vedan looked at them with understanding. "I know," he replied. "I never meant to ruin your birthdays, but the reason I chose those specific days to send the rings was that it was my only opportunity when both of your birthdays aligned perfectly. This alignment was influenced by the time distortion created by the vast distance between your planets." The weight of his words hung in the air, leaving Rachit and Ciona to ponder the significance of their shared fate.

"What do you mean…?" Vedan replied. "Both of you are situated at opposite edges of this universe, resulting in a significant gap between the timelines of your planets. Rachit, you reside on Planet Earth, which is currently in a phase where the universe has completed one-third of its expansion journey, close to the very beginning of that expansion. Meanwhile, Ciona comes from Planet Ferrosa, where the universe is nearing the end of its expansion phase, just before it begins to contract."

They countered, "What's the purpose behind these rings?"

Vedan held up his locket, which featured a ring that was distinctly different from the ones Rachit and Ciona possessed. "The reason I wear this ring, embedded in my locket, is that I am your superior. We have a greater purpose to fulfil."

Rachit and Ciona exchanged curious glances and replied hastily, "A purpose…? Who are we?"

Fig 5. Vedan unleashed his small amount of power, emitting a supersonic sound into the void to calm them.

6.
Sacred
Duty

Rachit and Ciona exchanged curious glances as Vedan began to explain their existence. "Let's start from the beginning," he said, setting the stage for a profound revelation. "We, along with my ring, are the creators of the universe. It's essential to understand that the four of us are required for this grand creation."

Rachit, puzzled, asked, "What do you mean by 'in real form'? Are we in fake forms right now?"

Vedan reassured him, "Don't misunderstand me; I'll clarify everything. Just have a little patience, kid."

He continued, "The universe is not what you perceive it to be. People on your planet, as well as those on others where life exists, believe that the universe is endlessly expanding. But that's not the whole truth. The universe has its own lifespan. After billions of years, it will face destruction, making way for a new universe to emerge. This cycle, which you might know as the Big Bang, occurs every 42 billion years. According to the religious beliefs on both your planets, you may have heard that the universe is merely a cycle of life, returning to its origin. These ideologies were instilled by the members of my organization, to help explain this cosmic reality."

Vedan continued, "Basically, we have been assigned certain duties related to the administration of the universe. My role involves creating the universe with the help of my ring, and I require your assistance in this monumental task. Additionally, I have superiors—those who created me—whom I must report back to."

Rachit and Ciona exchanged shocked looks. "People above you? An organization? Superiors? What on earth are you talking about?" they exclaimed in unison.

Vedan calmly replied, "I will explain all of that later. For now, let's focus on our primary task: the creation of the universe."

Rachit, still trying to piece everything together, asked Vedan, "So, are you saying that we are in the final period of the universe, which is why you called Ciona and me to help recreate it?"

Vedan nodded, "Exactly! I'm glad you're beginning to grasp the situation. However, we still have time to prepare for it."

Ciona interjected, "But you just said the universe is on the brink of extinction, and now you're telling us we have time to prepare?"

Rachit added, "Ciona's right. Can you please explain this more simply? All of this is just confusing us…"

Vedan replied, "Yes, the universe is indeed nearing its end, and I have called you at the perfect moment—your birthdays align at this time. Fortunately, I have enough time to teach you about the creation process so that you can learn it thoroughly."

Vedan continued, "Once you learn the process and make it the aim of your life, that will be the moment when you become worthy again and evolve into your true forms."

Ciona, filled with curiosity, questioned Vedan, "How will both of us contribute to the creation of the universe? Why don't we remember anything, and how is it that you recall every detail about us?"

Vedan responded confidently, "I am your Creator!!!"

Both Rachit and Ciona were taken aback, exclaiming in disbelief, "What???"

Vedan, undeterred by their shock, clarified, "Yes, dear ones, I am your Creator. Allow me to introduce you to your true forms, the ones that existed before and helped me in the creation of this current universe."

Vedan explained to Ciona and Rachit that he created them to help in the formation of this universe, just as his superior had created him. He explained to Rachit, "You provide the elements or any physical entity with its nature, whether it is strong or soft, hot or cold. Your role is to infuse life into things, or simply put, to give them a soul. Ciona, on the other hand, has the ability to shape the physical appearance of anything, be it water, stone, living creatures, or plants. However, until Rachit imbues these forms with a soul, they remain lifeless."

Ciona then asked Vedan how they would accomplish this, expressing her uncertainty by stating, "I have never done anything like this in my life."

Vedan responded, "I called both of you shortly before the end of the universe so that you could take your time to learn and prepare properly."

Then Rachit asked Vedan, "Why do you keep making us reincarnate? If you could keep us alive like you forever, then you wouldn't need to teach us repeatedly."

Vedan replied, "The universe doesn't work that way. Every time we create a new universe, it must have a distinct identity; it cannot be the same as the previous ones."

Ciona and Rachit asked, "Why is this necessary?"

Vedan replied, "First, you need to understand how your reincarnation works. Every time you successfully create new universes, being together with such power is a bit unsafe for the universe. If either of you were to manipulate your powers, it could change the reality of the universe and disrupt its timeline or path.

"So, whenever the purpose of both of you is fulfilled, you both go to different corners of a new universe and channel your energy into planets, which leads to the emergence of life in that universe. You both have to sacrifice yourselves to make life possible. Whether it's humans or aliens, you both are their ancestors. Then, from the planets where you provide your energy, life begins to flourish. All living beings gradually evolve and spread across different parts of the universe. When the universe reaches its end, that energy transforms into a physical form, and at this moment, that form is you two."

Rachit asked, "We haven't ventured beyond our solar system, yet you claim that various species on Earth emerged with the assistance of the energy from my previous version. How can this be possible? Please provide a more detailed explanation on this matter."

Ciona also agreed with him.

Vedan said, "Humans are not alone on Earth. Rachit, you must know that dinosaurs existed on Earth at one time, and there were many different species that were born both on Earth and on planets like Ciona, eventually settling elsewhere. However, energy always remains on the planets where you both have provided your energy, which is why you are here now."

Ciona asked, "How did you find us? I mean, how did you know which planet we would be on, and how did you determine that among so many beings, the energy resides in us?"

Vedan replied, "I don't know which planets you both are on; it always remains a mystery to ensure the safety of the universe. The task of finding you lies within these rings. These rings sense energy in its physical form. When the time comes for the universe to end, I awaken from my slumber and throw both rings into the cosmos, which always return to me with both of you."

Ciona and Rachit both asked Vedan about the necessity of each universe having a distinct identity.

Vedan said, "Yes, listen. My superiors say that it is essential for each universe to have its own distinct identity. Each rebirth in a universe must have its own identity, and this is only possible in one way: by both of you sacrificing yourselves to be reborn. This works in such a way that when energy transforms into any body, it possesses its own unique consciousness and a different way of thinking. This is what gives your ideas a distinct nature, which in turn provides your previous version of the universe with its own identity. The planets, stars, and space all depend on the creativity of your current versions. I will soon teach you how to create the basic elements, but how you both use those natural elements together will depend on you.

"Let me share with you the process of creating the elements of the universe, a sequence that has remained constant throughout each cycle of creation. It begins with Space, followed by Air, Fire, Water, and finally, Earth. You may have noticed that the symbol of Space is absent from your ring. This is because I will take the initiative to provide the necessary Space for you to create the other four elements within it. Both of you have pondered, 'Why don't we have the power to create Space?'

"Vedan wisely remarked, 'Power corrupts; absolute power corrupts absolutely.' This serves as a reminder that if either of you were to manipulate or misuse such power, it could lead to catastrophic disruptions in the universe. This is precisely why the ability to create Space is not granted to you.

"If any misconduct occurs with the powers you hold, there remains a chance for us to salvage the universe. However, if there is a breach concerning the powers associated with the creation of Space, it would be impossible for me or my superiors to prevent the universe from facing its demise. This is why I hold the position of your superior, and why I possess this locket, which is akin to your rings but serves a distinctly different purpose. My locket functions as a central source of energy, requiring you both to channel your powers into it. At the same time, I will also infuse it with my own energy. Once it has absorbed enough power and reaches its maximum capacity, it will erupt, creating a vast empty space. As you begin your work on the universe and the Space expands, the four elemental forces will gradually emerge. This phenomenon occurs because, while we are energizing my locket, the powers of the four elements that you hold, along with your rings, assist in directing that energy into the locket."

7.
Saga of Power and Love

After making them aware of their harsh reality, Vedan turned to them and said, "Hold my hand, kids." Vedan stood between them, with Ciona holding his right hand and Rachit holding his left. They noticed that Vedan was chanting some sort of incantations, his eyes closed, yet a glow emanated from within his eyelids. Suddenly, they found themselves teleported to a planet that appeared breathtakingly beautiful from space. The planet looked almost like Earth but resembled Ciona's home planet too, with lush green vegetation, blue waters, and some deserts spread across its surface.

"So coming straight to the point," Vedan began, "your training will take place here. Every fundamental aspect of space is present on this planet, i.e., air, fire, water, and earth (rock). That's the reason I have chosen this planet for you. Since everything is available here, you both can experiment on it by understanding each and every characteristic of it. This will help you to even explore all the angles of it. Also, keep one thing in your mind: in order to gain your original self and utilize its full potential, your energies have to be attached to each other. Individually, you both are powerful, but when you are passionate about each other, it will unleash your ultimate strength, and you both will be unstoppable."

Ciona asked Vedan, "How long will it take?"

Vedan replied, "Sometimes you learn quickly, and sometimes it takes time — it depends on how your mind has been shaped by the life you've lived so far, how you think, understand, and apply your knowledge. However, the most challenging and crucial part is for your thoughts to become one. Your thinking must sync to the extent that Rachit knows exactly what you are thinking and vice versa."

Vedan embraced them and made them calm, which gave them faith in themselves. He continued, "You both can do this, I have complete faith in you."

The three of them then descended to the planet. Rachit and Ciona were awestruck by its beauty, amazed that a place could be this magnificent purely because of nature. They saw animals, trees, plants, fruits, and flowers all around. Vedan, however, interrupted them, saying, "I didn't bring you here to admire the scenery. Everything you see here, feel it, learn to create it, and experiment with it. Let me explain the sequence of creation of the five elements: Space was created first, followed by Air, Fire, Water, and finally Earth, or what you might call Stone. I will teach you about the four elements, excluding Space, as you both don't possess the power to create it. Neither am I going to teach you about it. So I am leaving you both here, and I will come back in a week's time. Don't disappoint me, you are all what I have...!"

Rachit and Ciona walked together into the forest, admiring the sights and nature. Rachit asked, "Tell me something about yourself—what did you do on your planet, and how was it there?"

Ciona, being relaxed, responded, "On my planet, my father grew crops, which is what most families do. We also raised animals." She then asked, "Do people on your planet do the same?"

Rachit replied, "No, not at the place where I reside. This type of occupation is performed by the people in the countryside."

Ciona then asked, "Have you ever seen something beyond the skies before?"

Rachit answered, "No, I haven't. But there were great people who, after much effort and scientific advancements, managed to go beyond the skies. Some returned, while others didn't, but they shared everything they discovered. Today, our science has advanced to the point where we can observe these things from our homes. But what Vedan has shown us is something I never expected that I would ever see in my life."

Ciona agreed, "Yeah, that's true. Even I never thought that such events would occur in my life."

Ciona asked, "How many people are in your family?"

Rachit replied, "Just my mother and me. My father left my mother before I was born."

Ciona, feeling bad, said, "I'm sorry to hear that. Did you ever know why he left you both?"

Rachit, in a very low, sad voice, responded, "No."

Rachit shared his past about how their life was and how he and his mother had faced struggles. While speaking, Rachit's eyes became wet. Rachit's story touched Ciona's heart. She said, "Rachit, don't cry, dear, don't feel alone… I'm here with you…"

Ciona, trying to make him calm and happy again, gave him a warm hug and brought peace to him. When she hugged him, Rachit felt something different. He felt peace, and this feeling was something new to him. Even Ciona felt the same feeling. They were feeling connected, and this feeling made Rachit happy again.

Continuing their conversation, Rachit asked, "How about your family?"

Ciona answered, "We're a big family — two brothers, four sisters, and our parents."

Rachit, surprised, exclaimed, "Wow, quite a big family!"

They both laughed together. They kept walking and talking, getting to know each other. They were enjoying exploring various things in the forest. Night fell, and both Rachit and Ciona were exhausted. They lay on soft grass, being close to each other under the open sky, trying to sleep. However, the cold breeze made it hard for Ciona to fall asleep.

Rachit was randomly waving his hands in the air. In a matter of minutes, Ciona felt a hot breeze. When Rachit stopped waving his hand, the cold breeze started again. Ciona felt the change in temperature and told Rachit about it as he was unaware of it. Rachit was wondering about the situation. He then placed his hand on the ground and focused intently. Slowly, his palm began to glow, and the grass beneath started to warm up slightly. Rachit used his power for the first time.

Ciona felt the warmth in the ground and was even able to feel connected with nature. Ciona got a glimpse of her power. They both kept trying and learning more about the wonders they were able to do, and it was helping them gain confidence in their powers. Since some of their powers were unleashed, they were even feeling more connected to each other.

It was the middle of the night, and they were tired and dizzy. They sat on the ground holding each other's hands and were very happy. Soon their eyes closed, and they both were asleep. It was midnight, and both of them were in a good sleep. Gradually, Rachit was waving his hand in the air. He wasn't awake, but still, his hand was waving…

Rachit found himself floating in a dark space, surrounded by an unreal silence. Suddenly, he heard his mother's voice calling out to him and realized he was in his residence in Norway. He was astonished to hear his mother's voice, but he thought, how does his mother reach Norway, as she was in Mumbai? He rushed outside his apartment and started looking for her. He kept following the voice and found himself in a swarming market. He was pushing people aside in order to quench the thirst of his eyes as he had caught a glimpse of her on the other side of the place.

"Rachit! Rachit!" The sound kept getting louder as if she was crying out for help. He jolted awake, realizing it was just a dream. Yet, the haunting echoes of "Rachit! Rachit!" still lingered in his ears. As he looked around, he noticed that Ciona was not by his side, and the voice seemed to be coming from her. Driven by concern, Rachit began to run towards the source of the sound. Soon, he spotted Ciona, who appeared frightened and was looking in another direction.

Rachit rushed to her side, asking, "Are you okay?" Just then, he noticed what had her so alarmed—a massive creature resembling a blue sabretooth was preparing to pounce on them. In a panic, Rachit instinctively raised his hand to shield her from the impending attack. Their eyes closed in fear as they thought of a collision happening with that creature. To their surprise, they heard a "thud" sound as if something heavy had fallen on the ground. When they opened their eyes, the creature was unconscious.

Rachit asked again, "Are you okay?" She, being in an unstable state of mind, was not able to express how thankful she was to him. Without saying anything, she hugged Rachit tightly. Rachit, after a pause of a second, put his arms around her, making her calm and giving her comfort. The bond between Rachit and Ciona was getting stronger, and they were even more connected with each other now.

Ciona asked Rachit, "What was the sound of the thud? Where did it come from?"

Rachit himself was not aware of it, so he responded, "I don't know, Ciona. When I shielded you with my hand, I felt something, like something came out from my palm. We'll get back to it. Let's go to the creature first and check whether it's alive or not."

No matter that the creature was going to kill them, they still were affectionate for it. When Ciona placed her hand on it, she realized she couldn't feel its heartbeat. Ciona added, "You can bring it back to life."

Rachit replied, "But what if it attacks us again?"

Ciona reassured him, "You have the ability to change the emotions of powerful beings, just like you did last night by changing the temperature of the surroundings. You just changed its purpose. Besides, we came here to learn, so we need to train ourselves in some way."

Rachit placed his hand on the creature's head, closed his eyes, and concentrated, saying, "You are now a beloved and loyal creature of ours." His hand began to glow, and the creature came back to life. This time, it showed immense affection towards both Rachit and Ciona, behaving as if it were their pet.

Ciona extended her hand towards the creature, gently resting it on its head. As she did, her hand also started to glow, and gradually, the creature shrank in size. Finally, it transformed into a small, innocent animal. Seeing this, Ciona exclaimed, "Now you look so cute!" and both Rachit and Ciona burst into laughter.

Rachit said, "Let's name it Kigen."

Ciona liked the name but asked, "Does it have any meaning?"

Rachit replied, "This is our first creation, and in one of the languages from my planet, 'Kigen' means 'beginning.'"

Ciona smiled and responded, "That's wonderful!!!"

Finally, they got familiar with some of their powers.

Ciona said, "You remember about the thud sound."

Rachit responded, "Ooo yeah. Let me try again to see if it comes again."

Rachit started waving his hands in the air, but nothing happened. He was waving in every direction but still didn't get any result. While Rachit kept trying, Ciona was checking whether the sabretooth was alive or not. As Rachit kept trying, something came to his mind, so he put his palm towards a rock at a distance from him. He waited for a moment, and a repulsor light, a beam of power, came out from his palm and struck the rock. The rock shattered. Ciona was amazed.

From there, Rachit and Ciona's journey of learning the four elements began, gradually mastering each one. They engaged in various activities where they explored and learned about the characteristics of each element. They were also understanding the nature of the planet they were on, kept walking, kept going to new places, viewing beautiful scenarios, and learning about their characteristics and their purpose of existence on this planet.

Gradually, they started creating things, initially beginning with small things. Ciona created a rock-type object, and Rachit gave the rock its characteristics, like how hard it should be and its composition. Then Ciona made a small stream of water flowing nearby a river, and Rachit gave the stream its behaviour—whether it should be gentle flowing, aggressive flow, or flow with minor waves. In this manner, they kept creating various things and kept altering the things present in their surroundings. It helped them to know their powers and how to operate them.

Since they were working together, it was even helping their bond to grow and was strengthening the connection between them. As their confidence rose, they started practicing their powers on a bigger level, such as creating towering mountains and covering them with snow to enhance the beauty of their surroundings. They redirected rivers to shape the landscape where they wished to live and constructed a beautiful home, resembling a grand palace.

They explored the ocean, guiding the waves according to their desires. They changed the seasons at will, sometimes bringing rain and other times sunshine. They skilfully managed the fire in the forest, using it to create stunning fireworks at night. They cultivated different kinds of edible fruits and crops, ensuring a steady food supply. They maintained the life cycles of all living creatures to ensure the planet's survival and managed the flow of air as needed.

As they engaged in these activities over the course of about four to five months, Rachit and Ciona fell deeply in love. Their bond grew stronger, and they became so attuned to each other that they could sense each other's thoughts and feelings. Kigen also became important to them in their life as it became part of their life and a symbol of their first creation.

Suddenly, the sonorous sound of horns echoed through the sky. As Rachit and Ciona looked up, they saw Vedan approaching, soaring through the air. When Vedan landed before them, he exclaimed, "Very well! It seems you both have taken your time and learned to bend and alter each of the elements. Show me some examples!"

In response, Rachit and Ciona took Vedan to a desert. They held each other's hands tightly, closed their eyes, and focused. As they concentrated, their palms and closed eyes began to glow, and gradually, the sand in the desert started to vibrate. Dark clouds gathered in the sky, and a strong wind began to pick up. Before long, the wind escalated into a fierce storm, and heavy rain started to pour down. As the earthquake began, Vedan watched as the desert sand slowly transformed into fertile soil and rocky terrain. Gradually, grass began to sprout from the ground, and before long, the desert was transformed into a lush, fertile land filled with trees and plants, while the once-clear sky was now engulfed in a storm.

As they listened to Vedan, Rachit and Ciona began to grasp the profound significance of their powers—not just for their own benefit, but for every element surrounding them. Then Vedan turned to both of them with a satisfied smile and said, "Very good, I am pleased."

However, Rachit and Ciona, in perfect harmony, responded, "You have witnessed our powers, but you did not grasp the significance of the vision we shared."

Vedan cast a puzzled glance at the tumultuous skies swirling above, the vibrant green earth beneath his feet, and asked, "I don't understand anything."

In unison, they explained, "The very ground you stand upon embodies every element you urged us to master: AIR dances as the wind, WATER falls softly as rain, and EARTH transforms from sand to solid rock."

Vedan interjected, "And FIRE?"

Just then, a bolt of lightning struck a nearby tree, igniting it in a fierce blaze. With awe, Vedan remarked, "I have witnessed countless manifestations of your powers throughout time, but perhaps this is the first instance where you have displayed such strength and wisdom."

As his words hung in the air, the storm clouds began to part, revealing a clear sky, and Rachit and Ciona returned to their usual demeanour. Vedan continued, "Your powers are now far more focused and effectively utilized than in your previous forms. I urge you to cultivate this further so that the universe we create may garner the admiration of my superiors. To achieve this, you will need to pass a test."

With that, Vedan vanished into thin air. Rachit and Ciona shouted in desperation, "Vedan! Where are you? What test, Vedan…!?"

Fig 7. Rachit used his powers to soothe the surroundings for Ciona.

8.

Rebirth From Ashes

Rachit and Ciona were in a dreaded situation as Vedan left them no hint and just got disappeared. They kept looking for him around but there was no sign of him. The situation kept getting tense as few moments passed. The noiseless surrounding and the air flew faintly, there were no sounds of animals and rustling leaves, and not even the gentle flow of water. In this tense atmosphere, Kigen rushes towards Ciona, clinging to her in a panic, clearly frightened by the impending situation. Rachit can also sense Kigen's fear, noting the rapid beating of his heart and the trembling of his body. The current situation was heightening their anxiety as they were completely unaware about the upcoming events which would devastate their happiness.

Just then, a deafening sound rips through the sky, and as Rachit and Ciona look up, they see a massive meteor hurtling toward their planet at an alarming speed. "What the hell..!!!", Rachit spoke hastily. They both turned to each other and the expressions on their face indicated that they were in a state of shock. The meteor collided with the ground miles away leading to the creation of a shockwave which was felt far away from the collision spot. Even Rachit and Ciona felt it. "Rachit, how this is possible…Out of nowhere, how can a meteor entered into the atmosphere of this planet??" Rachit was sensing something huge coming around. Both heard a huge bang. It was the sound of two meteors who got smashed among each other, when both look above (in the sky) in the direction of sound, on having the sight of the visuals they lost faith in their eyes. The sky was full of tiny meteors breaking apart from their parent meteor. A vast meteor shower was about to unfold over their world which would destroy everything. Following the shower, a gigantic meteor was also approaching towards the planet. The sight of this meteor was so terrific that one might lose the sight of its eyes. Those flames with the shining fire balls of rock debris were like someone had revealed a pathway from the depths of hell to our planet. Gradually, the entire sky begins to change colour, transforming into a terrifying spectacle that resembles flames licking the heavens. Rachit and Ciona are consumed by worry, their bodies trembling in fear as their hearts race with anxiety. Rachit turns to Ciona and exclaims, "Vedan can't do this to us! Why would he want to completely destroy what we've transformed?!" Ciona responds, her voice filled with dread, "Despite everything we've done to prove ourselves, Vedan still wants to do this to us, he stills wants to test whether we are worthy or not." The weight of their situation hangs heavily in the air, making them feel an increase in their sense of fear and dread. The circumstances were making them believe that their doomsday was near.

Kigen was shivering on seeing the visuals. Ciona in a wavered sound spoke "Rachit, How are we gonna stop this?" Rachit replies, "If we don't stop this, then we wont have anything left to save...!" Rachit turned to Ciona and spoke in a very hard and rough voice "Let's not grieve, its not done yet. We both are capable as we possess the universal divine power this the power and lets show Vedan who the hell are we...! We won't let this calamity destroy our world. Whatever it takes..."

Ciona said "Can you feel the meteor? If you could match the weight of that massive meteor with the air, maybe we could slow it down and destroy it in the air only." Rachit responded "It's worth a try" Rachit concentrates with all his might but shakes his head in frustration, saying, "I don't know; the meteor won't let me feel it from within, that's why I can't sense it." Ciona presses him, "Try again!" He kept trying but the meteor didn't slowed even a second. Rachit thinks for a moment. Ciona spoke hastily "Lets try this, I will throw anything large towards the meteor, no matter how big it is. And you transform them into heavy rock objects" With determination, Ciona focuses and begins to hurl massive trees and uproot large stones from the ground, using her powers to launch them toward the meteor. Meanwhile, Rachit channelizes his abilities to transform each object into a diamond-like projectile, hoping that together they might shatter the meteor. However, as the makeshift weapons collide with the meteor, it becomes painfully clear that not a single scratch is made on its surface. But it helped to destroy some of the tiny meteors in the sky. The meteor continues its relentless descent, unaffected by their desperate attempts.

As the meteor draws closer to the planet, Rachit urges Ciona, "Use your powers to gather clouds in front of the meteor. I will strengthen them like a solid shield so that the meteor disintegrates in the air." Focusing intently, Ciona raises her hands to the sky, attempting to shape the clouds into a dense formation aimed at the meteor. As the clouds grow thicker in its path, she shouts, "Rachit! It's your turn now!"

With all his strength, Rachit transforms the clouds into a powerful iron-like barrier, holding them in place until the meteor collides with the wall they created. When the meteor strikes the metallic clouds, the barrier shatters into countless pieces, yet the meteor remains completely unscathed. Witnessing this, Rachit and Ciona feel their spirits plummet, left with nothing but despair as they can only watch the inevitable unfold before them.

The meteor collides with the planet about 30 to 40 miles away, creating a massive shockwave that ripples through the air. Ciona instinctively shields Kigen with her body. For a moment, everything seems still, but gradually the ground begins to tremble beneath them. Rachit's attention is focused on the smaller fragments of the meteor, worried they might fall on them. Just then, Ciona notices a bright light emanating from where the larger meteor has struck. With intense concentration, she tries to see what's happening, and suddenly, a massive wave of fire erupts from the impact site, slowly advancing toward Rachit and Ciona. Alarmed, Ciona screams, "Rachit! Run!" The sight of the approaching inferno sends a rush of adrenaline through Rachit, and he feels his heart race as he realizes the danger they are in.

Together, they try to run as fast as they can in the opposite direction. Rachit, Ciona, and Kigen — who is cradled in Ciona's arms — dash for their lives, but soon, fragments of the meteor begin to rain down from the sky. As they sprint, Rachit channels his powers to shield them from the falling debris, ensuring that no rocks harm them.

However, the flames from the impact quickly reach them. Rachit uses his abilities to cool the fire as it advances, but the intensity is overwhelming, and he starts to feel his strength waning. Seeing this, Ciona struggles to create a wall of earth around them, but she finds it increasingly difficult as she also has to protect Kigen. Meanwhile, small sparks break through Rachit's protective barrier, causing Ciona to worry as they threaten to harm them all. The situation grows dire, and the weight of their predicament presses heavily on her as she fights to keep them safe. But as Ciona puts all her strength into raising the wall, a piece of the meteor crashes down beside Rachit, Ciona, and Kigen. The impact causes Rachit and Ciona to stumble, while Kigen is thrown in the opposite direction. Rachit is severely injured but manages to maintain a protective barrier around himself and Ciona. However, due to Kigen's distance, he is unable to shield the child from the chaos.

When Ciona looks over at Kigen, she sees him engulfed in flames, alive but burning. The sight sends a shock through her; she feels as if she has become a lifeless shell, paralyzed by horror. Just then, the flames subside, and Rachit loses consciousness. As Ciona rises and surveys the surroundings, it appears as if the entire area has turned into a graveyard. There are no trees, no plants, no animals — only desolation, a barren land devoid of life, with not a single drop of water in sight.

Ciona's attention shifts to Rachit, who is in a near-unconscious state. She tries to lift him up and anxiously asks, "Rachit, wake up! Are you okay? Rachit! Rachit!" Although Rachit is barely conscious and attempts to respond, his weakness prevents any words from escaping his lips. In a moment of desperation, Ciona gathers a handful of sand from the ground and takes Rachit's hand, placing it within her own, which is filled with the sand. She urges him, "Just make this last attempt and read my mind; channel the energy I'm thinking of through this sand." Rachit concentrates, and for a brief moment, their hands begin to glow with a soft light, signifying a connection between them.

Ciona withdrew her hand from Rachit, and in that moment, she transformed into something akin to dry sand, merging with the vibrant green water around her. Then, she handed Rachit a strange liquid. For a while, nothing happened, but suddenly, Rachit began to tremble. Gradually, he started to scream, his heartbeat racing uncontrollably, and he became drenched in sweat. Out of nowhere, he let out a primal roar, his breath coming in short gasps as if a wild beast had entered the scene. He felt an overwhelming surge of power coursing through him, so intense that he feared his veins might burst. The adrenaline surged through him like a wild river, and he turned to Ciona, his eyes wide with disbelief and panic. "What have you made me drink?" he demanded, his voice a mix of fear and fury.

Ciona replied, "There's a plant at our home that my people drink before going hunting in the jungle. It energizes them and fills them with enthusiasm. I couldn't bear to see you in this state, so I had no other choice." As she spoke, tears began to stream down her face, and she continued, "Look at what Vedan has done to us. He has devastated our world beyond recognition." Rachit's anger soared to new heights for two reasons. First, the liquid Ciona had given him surged through his veins, filling him with an overwhelming strength that left him disoriented and unable to calm himself. Second, he was witnessing the destruction caused by Vedan's meteors for the first time, a sight that ignited his fury and helplessness. The chaos around him intensified, echoing the turmoil within as he grappled with both the newfound power and the devastation that surrounded them.

Rachit, filled with rage, surveyed the devastation around him, flames licking the sky in every direction. In that moment, he turned to Ciona, his voice charged with determination and fury. "We created this entire universe together, and losing our planet is not a big deal! Get up! We will restore everything!" As their minds connected in that intense moment, Ciona felt Rachit's passion igniting a fire within her as well. Gradually, she began to share in his fervour, realizing that together they had the strength to fix what had been broken. The shared anger and resolve fuelled their spirits, and they felt a growing conviction that they could reclaim their world and rebuild it from the ashes of destruction.

Ciona rises and says to Rachit, "Hold both my hands." As they grasp each other's hands tightly, they close their eyes and begin to meditate. Slowly, their palms start to glow, and the air around them begins to swirl with energy. The ground trembles beneath their feet. Rachit urges her, "Channel more power, Ciona!" In that moment, they feel themselves lifting off the ground, an exhilarating sensation like never before. Dark energy starts to flow from their palms, interspersed with tiny specks of white light. It's as if the entire planet is awakening, trembling like a toy in their hands. The earth cracks open, water surges forth, and massive mountains break free from the ground, slowly rising into the air. The world around them begins to transform, responding to their united strength and determination.

The sky begins to turn a deep blue where only devastation had once reigned, destroyed entirely by the meteor that had obliterated the atmosphere. Rivers start to form, flowing into ponds, which in turn connect to the oceans, creating a beautiful rebirth of the planet. Meanwhile, Vedan observes this breathtaking transformation from space, marvelling at the spectacle unfolding before him. "What a stunning sight," he whispers to himself, awestruck by the way the entire planet is being renewed. Despite having seen Rachit and Ciona in various forms before, there was something uniquely powerful about them this time. Gradually, life begins to flourish once again across the planet. Trees sprout, plants bloom, and fruits appear, while animals of all kinds emerge, filling the world with vibrancy and energy. The cycle of life is reignited, as nature reclaims its place, all thanks to the combined strength of Rachit and Ciona.

Rachit and Ciona slowly descend from the air, their hands returning to their original state. As their feet touch the soft grass, tears well up in their closed eyes. They open their eyes slowly, and the sight that greets them is so beautiful that it overwhelms them with joy. Rachit exclaims, "We did it, Ciona! We did it!" He bursts into laughter, and Ciona suddenly grabs Rachit, kissing him. They share a moment of love and happiness so intense that they are completely lost in each other, unaware of their surroundings. Vedan has already arrived and watches the scene unfold. Seeing them so engrossed in each other, he jokingly interrupts, "That's enough, guys," with a light chuckle. Ciona, upon noticing Vedan, gets angry and rushes towards him. However, Vedan reveals his hidden hand behind him, showing that it was actually Kigen. Ciona, surprised, looks at Kigen. Vedan apologizes, but before he can finish, Kigen jumps in and embraces

Ciona. The moment between them is filled with such warmth and affection that it seems to transcend words.

Rachit asks Vedan, "Why did you do that?" Vedan replies, "The last time you both showed me a scene, I had never seen anything like it before compared to your earlier versions. The way you both used your powers along with sharp intellect to alter the elements was commendable. But my greed held me back. I was greedy in thinking that you both were just a little short of perfection, so I chose a harsher path and tested you both. That's how I taught you how to use not just your powers and intellect, but also your emotions." Ciona says, "You could have taught us this by telling us!" Vedan replies beautifully, "Deceit leaves a mark that teaches a lesson for a lifetime and creates an impression that doesn't fade even when erased. That's why I chose this path. And I sent a meteor that was made of a substance you couldn't control or alter, so your powers wouldn't work against it. Alright, now you both have learned what you needed to learn, and you will have to come with me." Rachit and Ciona look at each other, realizing that their journey is now at a new turning point.

Fig 8. End of the World.

9.

Cosmos's

Last

Breath

Ciona stood on the edge of her home planet, her heart heavy with the weight of impending separation. Her eyes welled up with tears as she prepared to leave behind not just her beloved Kigen, but the place she had called home. The farewell was equally difficult for Rachit, whose words were filled with nostalgia for the beautiful moments spent at home.

"Go play, I'll be there in a bit," Ciona whispered to Kigen, her voice trembling. It was her way of concealing her sorrow, though she truly didn't want to say goodbye. Kigen, innocent and naïve, didn't comprehend that this was his last moment with Ciona.

Rachit placed a gentle hand on Kigen's head and murmured, "Goodbye my Champ." His voice carried the weight of his love and the difficulty of the farewell. Together, these moments highlighted the depth of their relationships, showing that sometimes, sacrifices are necessary for the ones we love.

As Vedan took flight, the journey symbolized a new beginning for Rachit and Ciona, but it was a heavy farewell nonetheless. They soared through the sky, gazing down at their planet, now appearing breathtakingly beautiful from such a height.

Suddenly, Ciona turned to Vedan, curiosity in her eyes. "Vedan, why aren't you teleporting us to the other side this time?"

Rachit supported her question, adding, "Yes, Vedan, Ciona is right. There must be a reason for this, and I feel like you're doing this for a purpose."

Vedan responded with a calm smile. "Yes, there is a reason behind this. You both have learned to create all the elements from the perspective of a planet, but now I want to show you the vastness of space. It is immense and profoundly calming to the eyes, allowing you to understand its grandeur. You both need to realize how far you must go with your powers to create a new universe."

As they continued their journey, the beauty of the cosmos unfolded around them, emphasizing the importance of their mission and the limitless potential that lay ahead. Vedan guided Rachit and Ciona through the wonders of the cosmos: first the planet, then the solar system, followed by galaxies, galaxy clusters, superclusters, the universe, and finally the observable universe.

Rachit and Ciona could hardly believe their eyes as they took in the magnificent sights before them. Massive planets, brightly shining stars, asteroids, and meteors raced through space, while enigmatic black holes loomed in the distance. Clouds of gas in various colours swirled gracefully, creating a breathtaking spectacle that soothed the eye.

They witnessed the birth and death of stars, phenomena known as nebulae and supernovae, as well as galaxies spinning like cosmic whirlpools. Overwhelmed by the grandeur of it all, Rachit exclaimed, "We truly have a great responsibility, Ciona."

Vedan reassured them, his tone steady and confident. "Don't worry; I never praise anyone without reason, and if I do, it means they are exceptional."

Hearing this, Rachit and Ciona felt a surge of motivation and excitement, ready to embrace the challenges ahead.

Then, stopping at a certain point, Vedan says, "Take one last look at the view until I count down from five." Rachit and Ciona quickly turn their gaze and begin the countdown, "5… 4… 3… 2… 1…" As they say "one," they snap their fingers, and the three of them find themselves in a vast, empty space where they can see countless galaxies appearing as tiny dots, many light-years away.

Rachit asks, "Why are these galaxies so far from us? I mean, why isn't there anything closer that we could reach?" Vedan replies, "This is my watch

point; from here, I can observe so much of space."
Just as he finishes speaking, Vedan places his hand
on his locket and suddenly disappears.

Seeing this, Rachit and Ciona feel a wave of
concern wash over them. They remember that the
last time Vedan vanished during a conversation,
something terrible had happened. In just a few
moments, Vedan reappears. Ciona, curious, asks,
"Where did you go? We both thought you might be
testing us again." With a light-hearted tone, Vedan
replies, "No, no, I went to my headquarters to initiate
the process of destruction for this universe."

Rachit interjects, "So, when you keep
mentioning your superiors or your headquarters, do
they really exist? Can we actually go there?" Vedan
responds, "Managing the cosmos is not as simple as
you think. You both only know one universe; we deal
with the multiverse. Where your understanding
ends, that's where our work begins. For now, these
conversations are not essential, and you have
nothing to do with these matters."

With a mind full of questions, Rachit presses
on, "Why don't you tell us more openly? After the
creation of our new universe, we won't even exist!"
Vedan, now slightly irritated, retorts, "I've already
said no; we're not discussing this topic anymore."
Then Vedan, calming his anger, says, "Quickly tell

me if you both see any commotion from a white light anywhere." With that, Vedan, Rachit, and Ciona start scanning their surroundings, running in search of the light as if they were in a race to see who could find it first. Suddenly, Ciona exclaims with excitement, "There it is!"

Vedan and Rachit turn to look in the direction she pointed. Vedan removes his locket, placing it between his hands, and begins to murmur something quietly. As he does this, his eyes and palms start to glow, mirroring the radiant glow in Rachit and Ciona's eyes and palms. Then, Vedan extracts his ring from the locket, and before their eyes, the ring begins to transform into a gyroscope-like shape, gradually becoming a light, spherical orb. With a determined gesture, Vedan throws the ring towards the direction of the light.

Vedan, with a serious yet gentle tone, looks at Rachit and Ciona and says, "This is the last moment of this universe; if you want to see or remember someone, you can say it now." The weight of the moment hangs in the air, and without hesitation, Rachit and Ciona reply in unison, "We want to see our family."

Understanding the significance of their request, Vedan takes both their hands in his, creating a bond that feels both comforting and protective.

"Close your eyes," he instructs softly, guiding them into a moment of reflection.

As they shut their eyes, a wave of warmth envelops them, and suddenly, Rachit and Ciona find themselves transported to a vivid scene of their families. Rachit's heart swells as he sees his mother, a whirlwind of activity, diligently engaged in household chores. The sight of her brings a smile to his face, but he's taken aback to discover that she has adopted a dog, a furry companion that seems to brighten her days. They share a joyful moment, a glimpse of happiness that resonates deeply within Rachit.

Meanwhile, Ciona's experience is equally poignant. She opens her eyes in her mind to see her younger siblings, who have grown noticeably. The passage of time feels different here, perhaps accelerated due to the time dilation on her planet. She gazes at her parents, longing to connect, and attempts to call out to them, but her voice is lost in the ether. Just then, she notices the clown sent by Vedan, who is engaging joyfully with her mom and dad, bringing laughter and light to their faces. This sight tugs at her heartstrings, and she fights to hold back the swell of emotions that threatens to overflow.

As the moments pass, Vedan gently releases their hands. The visions of their families begin to fade, like the last rays of sunlight at dusk. Rachit, feeling a sense of urgency, pleads, "Just a little longer, let us see."

Vedan, ever the guide, replies with a sense of finality, "Time is running out now, but always remember the happiness of both of you." His words linger in the air, a reminder of the love and joy they hold in their hearts, even as the universe around them shifts.

Rachit and Ciona watch intently as the white light gradually expands, slowly taking on the shape of an eye. Everything around them seems to be drawn toward this mesmerizing eye, as if it is absorbing the entire surroundings. With a sense of curiosity, Rachit asks, "Can we see it up close?" In an instant, Vedan teleports them right next to the white eye, where they can observe how each tiny speck of space is being pulled into it, as if it is opening a gateway to an extraordinary realm.

Ciona asks, "Why aren't we being pulled inside?" Vedan chuckles and replies, "It's my blessing." Massive galaxies, enormous planets, stars, and black holes are being drawn into the eye as if they no longer possess any weight or energy. They appear to be hollow objects, effortlessly pulled in. The white eye resembles a portal, with the entire universe being drawn into it from both sides.

Vedan comments, "So far, only the objects in space have been drawn in; now watch how the entire black void begins to be pulled in." Suddenly, a powerful flash of light bursts forth from within the eye, creating a blinding glare that envelops Ciona and Rachit. As they manage to steady themselves and look back, they see the black space being drawn in from the pointed corners of the eye, as if a velvet fabric is being swiftly gathered by an unseen force from within.

Upon closer observation, Rachit notices that while everything else in space is being drawn into the eye, the black space is accumulating into a small spherical object right at the centre of the eye. Rachit asks Vedan, "Why is all this space gathering in just that one spot and not being pulled in like everything else?" Vedan explains, "The object it's collecting in is my ring, which contains a unique pocket dimension where all this space is gathered for reuse."

Rachit, still a bit confused, responds, "Can you explain that in simpler terms?" Vedan smiles and replies, "Think of it this way: we are in a school. You two are the students, and I am the teacher, with my superior being the principal. The principal has provided each class with a blackboard. Now, if I, as the teacher, ask you to write something on the blackboard, you would write according to your understanding and then leave. I wouldn't bring in a new board; instead, I would just wipe it clean with an eraser and use it again."

As they watch, Rachit and Ciona feel the eye expanding, with the surrounding space becoming almost entirely empty. In a sudden jolt, the eye fully expands. They realize they are back in the same white void where they first met. Rachit tries to say something to Vedan, but his voice fails him. Vedan communicates through telepathy, saying, "Forget it; there is no space left, and now there is no sound either."

Then, Vedan's ring appears. He extends his hand, and the ring comes to rest in his palm. It still retains the shape of a gyroscope, but within its centre, a dark object spins slowly. Vedan addresses Rachit and Ciona, saying, "Can you imagine that the entire emptiness is now in my hands? Now it's our turn." With that, the three of them embrace, ready for a new beginning.

Fig 9. The contraction of the empty space in the ring.

10.
End is
The
New
Beginning

The whole universe had disappeared, as if the vast universe was meaningless. But it didn't seem that way; it looked like all three were in a white room with no end. Thinking about all this, Rachit asked Vedan one last time, "Why do we keep recreating this again and again? When if we want, we can create it once and maintain it well forever, so it can last for infinite years."

Vedan replied, "I don't have an answer to that, and I can't tell you much more. But I can tell you one thing, but you'll have to understand it yourself."

"What is it, Vedan?" Rachit asked.

Vedan said, "The reality is that we are characters in someone else's dreams. And if that person keeps dreaming the same dream over and over, perhaps the thought won't progress. Because to bring about any kind of revolution, a dream is essential, which shows us a new path for our thoughts, so that progress can happen."

Ciona also felt a deep connection to this idea, but without the full context, she couldn't grasp it as well as Rachit did. Still, both of them decided to trust Vedan.

Vedan said, "Rachit and Ciona, both of you extend the hand where you have worn your rings and place it on each other's hands."

They both brought their right hands forward, with Ciona placing her hand on top of Rachit's. Vedan then placed his ring, which had an empty space within it, on Ciona's hand. He instructed them, "No matter what, do not remove your hands from there."

Then, Vedan closed his eyes and began to form different gestures with his hands. Finally, he joined his palms together and started chanting some mantras. In an instant, he began to transform completely into a radiant white light. The white glow emanating from his hands gradually spread over his entire body, while Vedan's ring started to move as well.

Rachit and Ciona watched in awe, feeling a bit scared yet mesmerized by the sight before them. As Vedan's body continued to transform into radiant white light, his ring slowly began to lift off into the air.

Ciona's attention was drawn to his hand, as it was positioned the highest, and she noticed that gold was gradually filling the empty space in his ring.

Vedan had almost completely turned into this brilliant white light, and as his form became entirely luminous, it seemed as though he had vanished from sight.

The ring, now floating above Rachit and Ciona, began to move erratically before suddenly becoming still. In that instant, a blast-like energy surged from within the ring, causing Rachit and Ciona to instinctively close their eyes in fear. Yet, despite their terror, neither of them dared to remove their hands from the spot. They remained steadfast, determined to hold on, even as the unknown unfolded around them. Rachit and Ciona slowly opened their eyes, but they were initially blinded by a very bright light. As the scene cleared, they saw a person in front of them glowing with white light, but everything around them was pitch black.

Rachit asked the bright figure, "Vedan? Is that you?"

The response came, "Yes, Rachit, this is my true form. I just took this shape to make you both feel comfortable so you could quickly adapt to my presence."

Ciona, noticing the surrounding darkness, asked Vedan, "Is this what I was thinking?"

Vedan replied, "Yes, absolutely. We are in an empty space where we will create a new world."

Rachit remembered that while all this was happening, Ciona's ring was shining with gold, and perhaps her own ring was shining as well. As Rachit extended both his hands, he felt a shock because gold had also appeared on his ring. At the same time, Rachit's hands had turned dark up to his wrists, with sparkling stars shining on them.

Ciona gazed down at her hands, and to her astonishment, they mirrored the dark hue of her wrists, creating an eerie yet fascinating sight. Confusion flooded her mind, prompting her to turn to Vedan with a question that lingered in the air, "What has happened to our hands, Vedan? Is this our true form?"

Vedan, with a calm demeanor, reassured her, "You are absolutely right, but it's not time yet. As you both begin to harness your powers to create a new universe, your physical forms will gradually transform to reflect the essence of your hands."

Rachit, intrigued by Vedan's ethereal presence, inquired, "You appear just like white light, but why do we look like this?"

Vedan's eyes glimmered with wisdom as he explained, "The one who created me exists beyond the universe, wielding a power that transcends all measurements. That's why I am entirely white, embodying the purest form of energy, a force that exists beyond this universe. You both, on the other hand, are manifestations of this universe, which is why your skin bears this inky color. I fashioned you both as reflections of my powers, hence the small white dots scattered across your forms. If you observe closely, your bodies resemble a universe in themselves, with dark expanses and sparkling stars, each element a testament to the vastness of existence."

Vedan instructed Rachit and Ciona to step back a little from each other and extended his hand forward. In that moment, his ring, which once held the vastness of space, was revealed to be completely empty now. Vedan carefully sent his ring between Rachit and Ciona, asking them, "Are you ready?"

In unison, they responded, "Yes!"

Vedan then continued, "Close your eyes and focus solely on my voice. You must channel all your energy into this ring, which has four distinct bands, each representing an element. As you each contribute your energy, the power of the elements will flow into the ring. With each element you infuse, the layers of the ring will begin to unfold, revealing its true potential. What will happen at the end, I will explain to you both, but for now, concentrate on my voice."

The atmosphere around them shifted as they prepared to embark on this extraordinary journey, the air thick with anticipation and the promise of transformation.

Rachit and Ciona extended their hands toward Vedan's ring and closed their eyes. Vedan began to guide them with his voice, saying, "Feel each element deeply and recreate it in your minds. First, focus on the air, then move on to water, and finally, earth. Concentrate fully."

As Vedan encouraged Rachit and Ciona to embody each element, their true essence, which initially began to emanate from their hands, gradually enveloped their entire bodies. Vedan continued, "Remember how you both created air on the planet, forming an atmosphere that allowed life to thrive. Picture the waves of energy that enabled communication and supported the survival of living beings. Recall the fire and its brightness, a force of both destruction and life. Remember the water, its coolness, the very source from which life emerged. And finally, think of the earth, its solidity, the foundation that has allowed life to endure for centuries."

The atmosphere was charged with energy as they immersed themselves in these vivid memories, drawing strength from the elements they were channeling. As Vedan continued guiding them, Rachit and Ciona fully transformed into their true forms. Vedan instructed, "Open your eyes and channel all your inner strength with full dedication."

As they opened their eyes, a brilliant white light radiated from them, and they began to pour all their energy into the rings on their fingers. Beams of energy, like lasers, burst forth from their hands, merging into the rings. In an instant, the upper layers of the rings started to unfold, revealing the first shockwave, a soft white glow.

Vedan encouraged them, saying, "There are three more layers to go; I need more power!"

Rachit and Ciona began to chant, and before long, the second layer of the ring opened, releasing a vibrant yellow shockwave. Vedan, sensing the need for more intensity, remarked, "This isn't impressive;

I didn't expect this from you two. Put in more effort!"

Gradually, the sound of Rachit and Ciona's chanting grew louder, and the white spots within them started to shine brighter, fueling their determination to unleash the full potential of their powers. Vedan felt a wave of happiness within himself as he realized that the three of them were indeed on the right path.

Suddenly, the third layer of the ring burst open, releasing a stunning blue shockwave. Vedan shouted, "Just one last layer! Give it everything you've got!"

Rachit and Ciona began to scream, channeling every ounce of energy from within. The intensity radiating from them was so powerful that Vedan could hardly believe his eyes at the sight before him. As they continued to push their limits, the final small layer shattered, unleashing a vibrant brown shockwave that filled the air with raw energy. The atmosphere crackled with the force of their combined strength, marking a significant moment in their journey.

Rachit and Ciona paused to take in the sight before them: the ring had fully opened, resembling a golden flower in bloom. Above it, a small, glowing sphere of energy shifted colors, floating gently. As Rachit and Ciona stepped closer, the energy suddenly erupted in a blast. Instinctively, they shielded themselves with their hands and closed their eyes tightly, bracing for impact. A loud sound reverberated around them, and then, just as abruptly, silence fell.

When they finally opened their eyes, they discovered that the energy had vanished, and the three of them—Rachit, Ciona, and Vedan—had returned to their original forms. Confused, Rachit and Ciona simultaneously asked Vedan, "Where did the energy go? It just exploded right in front of us!"

In response, Rachit and Ciona positioned themselves directly in front of Vedan, and he pointed behind them with his finger, indicating something unseen. The air was thick with anticipation as they prepared to uncover the mystery of what lay beyond. As Rachit and Ciona turned to look, they saw a solitary white light shining brightly in the vastness of space, gradually growing larger.

Rachit asked Vedan, "What is that?"

Vedan replied in a single word, "BIG….. BANG…..!"

Rachit and Ciona could hardly believe their eyes as a new universe began to take shape right before them, born from their very presence. Vedan explained, "To witness this spectacle, I teleported both of you a short distance away at the moment of the Big Bang, allowing you to see how life emerges."

The light continued to expand, racing toward them faster than anything they had ever experienced. Gradually, they began to see the outlines of space within the circle of light. Suddenly, a shockwave from the Big Bang reached all three of them, transforming the once black void into a shimmering expanse filled with vibrant colors. The sight was breathtaking, and for the first time, Rachit and Ciona felt an overwhelming sense of divinity, realizing that they were, in essence, part of something far greater — something divine.

The shimmering stars were beginning to take shape, their formations mesmerizing to behold. Due to the reactions of gases and air, new types of space clouds were forming, swirling and shifting in the vastness of the cosmos. Tiny stones were gradually taking shape from the water particles and dust expelled by the stars.

Ciona, captivated by the spectacle, turned to Vedan and asked, "Can I see this up close?"

Vedan smiled and replied, "Yes! Absolutely! This is your creation; go ahead without hesitation."

With excitement, Ciona floated through space, moving closer to observe the formation of a star. Meanwhile, Vedan turned to Rachit and encouraged him, "You should go too; take a look."

Rachit shook his head, saying, "No, I'm fine here. The view is just as beautiful from where I am."

Vedan nodded in agreement and said, "That's a valid point. Alright, Rachit, what should I say…" Just as he was speaking, Vedan suddenly fell silent, as if lost in thought.

Rachit began calling out, "Vedan! Vedan!" He looked around, searching for Vedan, who had suddenly vanished while they were talking.

Meanwhile, Ciona was observing a star forming in a brilliant blue hue. Suddenly, strange flickering lights appeared within it, and the star began to emit its fiery tendrils. Feeling uneasy, Ciona instinctively pulled back, thinking it might be part of the star formation process.

Just then, Vedan reappeared beside Rachit, drenched in sweat and clearly shaken. His gaze quickly fell on Ciona, and he shouted, "Ciona…!"

As Ciona turned at the sound of his voice, the star unexpectedly plunged into a wormhole, pulling her in along with it.

Rachit couldn't believe his eyes; he turned to Vedan, panic rising in his voice, "Vedan! Where did Ciona go? Say something! Where is Ciona? Vedan…!"

In that moment, the vastness of the universe unfolded before them, revealing a wide view where they could see the universe itself had stopped expanding. Yet, the whereabouts of Ciona remained a mystery, leaving them both in a state of confusion and fear.

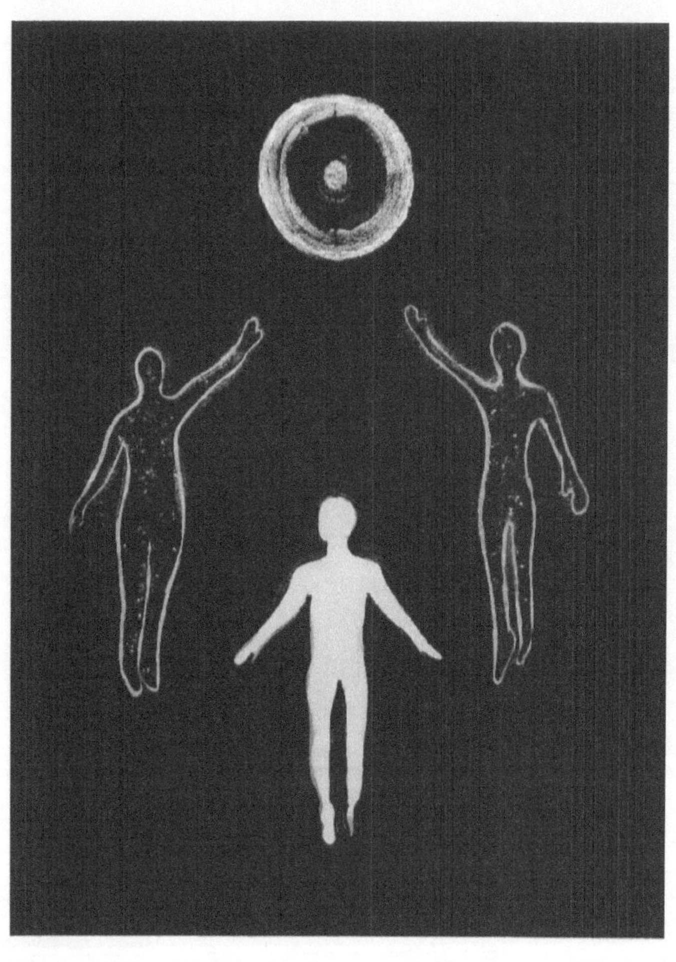

Fig 10. Time for recreation.

11.
Is this
The End
Of their
Journey?

As Vedan suddenly disappeared, we saw that he had arrived at his headquarters. Upon entering, he noticed, strangely, that there were no guards in the teleportation chamber, which was unusual. As he stepped out of the teleportation chamber, he was astonished to find that the entire headquarters was constructed entirely of gold. The building had a circular design, and in front of him was a grand gallery adorned with vertical lines through which energy flowed. There were so many lines that it was impossible to count them all.

Vedan was observing all of this casually when suddenly, he felt a sharp shove from behind. Turning around, he saw a figure clad in dark green armour, wielding a sword and preparing to attack him. As Vedan instinctively tried to defend himself, the armoured assailant was struck through the abdomen by a sword, and he collapsed lifelessly to the ground. Behind him stood a soldier in white and gold armour, who urgently called out to Vedan, "Hurry! Get to your control room!"

In a state of fear, Vedan sprinted towards the control room. Once inside, he was met with chaos; a fierce battle raged between the soldiers in green armour and his own troops. On the monitors, Vedan could see images of his entire universe displayed, adding to the gravity of the situation. Vedan averted his gaze and noticed that during the chaos, a soldier in green armour had swung his sword at the portal creation button, causing the system to malfunction. Suddenly, the monitor displayed a portal forming between Vedan's universe and an unknown one.

In a rush, Vedan dashed to the teleportation chamber, and as he arrived, he saw that the portal had already opened, pulling Ciona into it. Then, we were given a wide view of the entire universe. It had stopped expanding because the energies of both Rachit and Ciona were essential for the universe's expansion. With Ciona's departure, the universe had ceased to grow. Witnessing this, Vedan fell into a state of shock.

It was then that Rachit, realizing the gravity of the situation, brought Vedan back to his senses and urgently asked, "Where is Ciona?"

Vedan, still in disbelief, replied, "Huh?"

Rachit, growing increasingly frustrated, shook Vedan more forcefully and demanded, "Where did Ciona go!?"

Vedan responded helplessly, "I don't know."

After the Big Bang, Vedan's ring had returned to him, and it began to spin around his fingers. Vedan turned to Rachit and urged, "Quick, grab my hand!" As soon as Rachit took hold of

Vedan's hand, the two of them were instantly teleported away, leaving behind a profound silence.

The universe that Vedan, Rachit, and Ciona had created was now in a state of disarray, teetering on the brink of collapse. What would happen next remained uncertain, but soon enough, the answers would reveal themselves.

Fig 11. Vedan viewing the timelines in his HQ.

Illustration